Gypsy F

BOOK ONE
Illustrated Edition

COMPILED AND EDITED BY

FRANCIS HINDES GROOME

ILLUSTRATED BY

MAGGIE GUNZEL

ORIGINALLY PUBLISHED

BY

HURST AND BLACKETT, LONDON

[1899]

* * * * * * *

REPUBLISHED BY

ABELA PUBLISHING, LONDON

[2012]

Gypsy Folk Tales - Book One
Illustrated Edition

Abela Publishing,
London
United Kingdom
2012

ISBN-13: 978-1-907256-07-3

email Books@AbelaPublishing.com

www.AbelaPublishing.com/gypsytales1-ill

Frontispiece:
The Gypsy and the Vampire

Dedication & Philanthropy

This book is dedicated to the teachers and storytellers

who keep folklore and history alive

through the telling and re-telling of these tales

A percentage of the net from the sale of this book

will be donated to

THE RELIEF FUND FOR ROMANIA

Acknowledgements

The Publisher acknowledges the work that

FRANCIS HINDES GROOME

did

in compiling a collection of

GYPSY FOLK TALES

in a time well before any electronic media was in use.

Also, thanks to

MAGGIE GUNZEL

for the many hours spent illustrating this book.

'PAZORRHUS'

I AM no folklorist; I have merely dabbled in folklore as a branch of the great Egyptian Question, which includes also intricate problems of philology, ethnology, craniology, archæology, history, music, and what not besides. But for twenty years I have been trying to interest folklorists in Gypsy folk-tales. Vainly so far; and during those twenty years there have died Dr. Paspati, Dr. Barbu Constantinescu, Dr. Franz von Miklosich, Dr. Isidore Kopernicki, M. Paul Bataillard, and John Roberts, the Welsh-Gypsy harper: with them much has perished that folklorists should not have willingly let go. Meanwhile, however, a Rómani Grimm has arisen in Mr. John Sampson, the librarian of University College, Liverpool. With unparalleled generosity he has placed his collections at my free disposal--I trust I have not made too lavish use of them,--and has read, moreover, every page of the proofs of this volume, enriching it from the depths of his knowledge of 'matters of Egypt.' Another, a very old friend, to whom my debt is great, is the Rev. Thomas Davidson, author of the admirable folklore articles in *Chambers's Encyclopædia*; he has lent me scores of scarce works from his unrivalled folklore library. Others to whom I owe acknowledgments are: Mr. Tom Taylor, Mr. W. R. S. Ralston, Mr. W. A. Clouston, Dr. Hyde Clarke, Professor Bensly (all five also dead), Mrs. Gomme, Mr. H. Browne of Bucharest, Mr. Robert Burns, Lord Archibald Campbell, Mr. Archibald Constable, Mr. H. T. Crofton, Professor Dobschütz of Jena, Mr. Fitzedward Hall, Dean

Kitchin, Mr. William Larminie, Mr. David MacRitchie, M. Omont of the Bibliothèque Nationale, Dr. David Patrick, Dr. Fearon Ranking, Mr. Rufus B. Richardson of Athens, Professor Sayce, and Dr. Rudolf von Sowa of Brünn. And, finally, I would thank in advance whoever may send me corrections, additions, or suggestions on the subject of Gypsy folk-tales.

FRANCIS HINDES GROOME.
137 WARRENDER PARK ROAD,
EDINBURGH.

Publishers Note

In FHG's original work are fifty-eight introductory chapters giving a detailed background and history of the Gypsy peoples from around the world.
As our objective was to produce a volume of Gypsy folk tales, which would be just that, we have elected to include only three of those introductory chapters as background information.

In his original work, Francis Hindes Groome published seventy-six Gypsy folk stories. In order to keep the work to a more manageable and affordable size, we have elected to spilt the original volume into two volumes, each containing thirty-six stories.

John Halsted
Abela Publishing

BOOK ONE

Tales and stories from

Turkish Gypsies

Roumanian Gypsies

and

Bukowina Gypsies

CONTENTS

LIST OF ILLUSTRATIONS

INTRODUCTION

DISTRIBUTION OF GYPSIES.

No race is more widely scattered over the earth's surface than the Gypsies; the very Jews are less ubiquitous. Go where one will in Europe, one comes upon Gypsies everywhere--from Finland to Sicily, from the shores of the Bosporus to the Atlantic seaboard. Something under a million is their probable number in Europe; of these Hungary claims 275,000, Roumania 200,000, Servia 38,000, and Bulgaria 52,000. How many Gypsies there are in Great Britain I have not the vaguest notion, for there are no statistics of the slightest value to go by.[1] But I have never lived for any length of time in any place--and I have stayed in most parts of both England and Scotland--without lighting sooner or later on nomadic or house-dwelling Gypsies. London and all round London, the whole Thames valley as high at least as Oxford, the Black Country, Bristol, Manchester, Liverpool, and Yarmouth, it is here I should chiefly look for settled Gypsies. Whilst from study of parish registers, local histories, and suchlike, and from my own knowledge, I doubt if there is the parish between Land's End and John o' Groats where Gypsies have not pitched their camp some time or other in the course of the last four centuries.

---

[1] According to the *Spectator* (24th December 1897) ten thousand Gypsies wintered in Surrey in 1896-97!

Asia has untold thousands of these wanderers, in Anatolia, Syria, Armenia, Persia, Turkestan, and Siberia, perhaps also India and China; so, too, has Africa, in Egypt, Algeria, Darfûr, and Kordofan. We find them in both the Americas, from Pictou in Canada to Rio in Brazil; nor are New Zealand and Australia without at least their isolated bands.

To-day at any rate the sedentary Gypsies must greatly outnumber the nomadic: in Hungary only 9000, or less than one-thirtieth of the entire number, are returned as 'constantly on the move.' Still the race has always been largely a migratory race; its wide distribution is due to bygone migrations. Of these the most important known to us is that of the first half of the fifteenth century, whose movements have been so lovingly and laboriously traced by the late M. Paul Bataillard in his *Dè l'Apparition et de la Dispersion des Bohémiens en Europe* (1844), *Nouvelles Recherches* (1849), and 'Immigration of the Gypsies into Western Europe in the Fifteenth Century' (*Gypsy Lore Journal*, April 1889 to January 1890, for pages).

STORY-TELLING A LIVING GYPSY ART.

A tree can never be quite dead as long as it puts forth shoots; I fancy the very latest shoot in the whole Yggdrasil of European folk-tales is the episode in 'The Tinker and his Wife', where the tinker buys a barrel of beer, and says, 'Now, my wench, you make the biggest penny out of it as ever you can,' and she goes and sells the whole barrel to a packman for one of the old big pennies. That episode cannot be earlier than the introduction of the new bronze coinage in 1861; it looks as though it must itself be a recent coinage of Cornelius Price, or of Nebuchanēzar, his uncle. But, there, I have known a Gypsy girl dash off what was almost a folk-tale impromptu. She had been to a pic-nic in a four-in-hand, with 'a lot o' real tip-top gentry'; and '*Reía,*' she said to me afterwards, 'I'll tell you the comicalest thing as ever was. We'd pulled up, to put the brake on and there was a *púro hotchiwítchi* (old hedgehog) come and looked at us through the hedge, looked at me hard. I could see he 'd his eye upon me. And home he'd go, that old hedgehog, to his wife, and "Missus," he'd say, "what d' ye think? I seen a little Gypsy gal just now in a coach and four bosses"; and "*Dábla!*" she 'd say, "*sawkúmni 'as vardé kenáw*"' (Bless us! every one now keeps a carriage).

THEORY

To recapitulate, my theory, then, is this:--The Gypsies quitted India at an unknown date, probably taking with them some scores of Indian folk-tales, as they certainly took with them many hundreds of Indian words. By way of Persia and Armenia, they arrived in the Greek-speaking Balkan Peninsula, and tarried there for several centuries, probably disseminating their Indian folk-tales, and themselves picking up Greek folk-tales, as they certainly gave Greek the Rómani word *bakht,* 'fortune,' and borrowed from it *paramísi,* 'story,' and about a hundred more terms. From the Balkan Peninsula they have spread since 1417, or possibly earlier, to Siberia, Norway, Scotland, Wales, Spain, Brazil, and the countries between, everywhere probably disseminating the folk-tales they started with and those they picked up by the way, and everywhere probably adding to their store. Thus, I take it, they picked up the complete Rhampsinitus story in the Balkan Peninsula, and carried it thence to Roumania and Scotland; in Scotland, if John MacDonald was any sort of a Gypsy, they seem to have picked up 'Osean after the Feen.'

It is not so smooth and rounded a theory as I hoped to be able to present to folklorists, or as I might easily have made it by suppressing a little here and filling out somewhat there. But at least I have pointed out a few fresh parallels; I have, thanks to Mr. Sampson's generosity, enriched our stock, not of English folk-tales, but of folk-tales collected in England and Wales; and I have, I hope, stimulated a measure of curiosity in the strange, likeable, uncanny race, whom 'Hans Breitmann' has happily designated 'the Colporteurs of Folklore.' I let my little theory go reluctantly, but invite the fullest argument and discussion. There is nothing like argument. I was once at a meeting of a Learned Society, where a friend of mine read a most admirable paper. Then uprose another member of that Learned Society, and challenged his every contention. In a rich, sonorous voice he thus began: 'Max Müller has said (and I agree with Max Müller), that Sanskrit in dying left twins--Chinese and Semitic.'

F.H.G.

CHAPTER I

TURKISH-GYPSY STORIES

No. 1.--The Dead Man's Gratitude

A KING had three sons. He gave the youngest a hundred thousand piastres; he gave the same to the eldest son and to the middle one. The youngest arose, he took the road; wherever he found poor folk he gave money; here, there, he gave it away; he spent the money. His eldest brother went, had ships built to make money. And the middle one went, had shops built. They came to their father.

'What have you done, my son?'

'I have built ships.'

To the youngest, 'You, what have you done?'

'I? every poor man I found, I gave him money; and for poor girls I paid the cost of their marriage.'

The king said, 'My youngest son will care well for the poor. Take another hundred thousand piastres.'

The lad departed. Here, there, he spent his money; twelve piastres remained to him. Some bandits dug up a corpse and beat it.

'What do you want of him, that you are beating him?'

'Twelve piastres we want of him.'

'I'll give you them if you will let him be.'

He gave the money, they let the dead man be. He arose and departed. As the lad goes the dead man followed him. 'Where go you?' the dead man asked.

'I am going for a walk.'

'I'll come too; we'll go together; we will be partners.'

'So be it.'

'Come, I will bring you to a certain place.'

He took and brought him to a village. There was a girl, takes a husband, lies with him; by dawn next day the husbands are dead.

'I will hide you somewhere; I will get you a girl; but we shall always be partners.'

He found the girl (a dragon came out of her mouth).

'And this night when you go to bed, I too will lie there.'

He took his sword, he went near them. The lad said, 'That will never do. If you want her, do you take the girl.'

'Are we not partners? You, do you sleep with her; I also, I will sleep here.'

At midnight he sees the girl open her mouth; the dragon came forth; he drew his sword; he cut off its three heads; he put the heads in his bosom; he lay down; he fell asleep. Next morning the girl arose, and sees the man her husband living by her side. They told the girl's father. 'To-day your daughter has seen dawn break with her husband.'

'That will be the son-in-law,' said the father.

The lad took the girl; he is going to his father.

'Come,' said the dead man, 'let's divide the money.' They fell to dividing it.

'We have divided the money; let us also divide your wife.'

The lad said, 'How divide her? If you want her, take her.'

'I won't take her; we'll divide.'

'How divide?' said the lad.

The dead man said, 'I, I will divide.'

The dead man seized her; he bound her knees. 'Do you catch hold of one foot, I'll take the other.'

Out of her mouth fell a dragon

He raised his sword to strike the girl. In her fright the girl opened her mouth, and cried, and out of her mouth fell a dragon. The dead man said to the lad, 'I am not for a wife, I am not for any money. These dragon's heads are what devoured the men. Take her; the girl shall be yours, the money shall be yours. You did me a kindness; I also have done you one.'

'What kindness did I do you?' asked the lad.

'You took me from the hands of the bandits.'

The dead man departed to his place, and the lad took his wife, went to his father.

No. 2.--Baldpate

In those days there was a man built a galleon; he manned her; he would go from the White Sea to the Black Sea. He landed at a village to take in water; there he saw four or five boys playing. One of them was bald. He called him. 'Where's the water?' he asked. Baldpate showed him; he took in water.

'Wilt come with me?'

'I will, but I've a mother.'

'Let's go to your mother.' They went to her.

'Will you give me this boy?'

'I will.'

The captain paid a month's wages; he took the lad. They weighed anchor; they came to a large village; they landed to take in water.

The king's son went out for a walk, and he sees a dervish with a girl's portrait for sale. The king's son bought it; it was very lovely. The girl's father had been working at it for seven years. The king's son set it on the fountain, thinking, Some one of those who come to drink the water will say, 'I've seen that girl.' The captain came ashore; he took in water; he lifted up his eyes, and saw the portrait.

'What a beauty!' He went aboard, and said to his crew, 'There's a beauty yonder, I've never seen her like.'

Baldpate said, 'I'm going to see.'

Baldpate went. The moment he saw the portrait, he burst out laughing. 'It's the dervish's daughter. How do they come by her?'

Hardly had he said it when they seized him and brought him to the palace. Baldpate lost his head the moment they seized him. But two days later they came to him: 'This girl, do you know her?'

'Know her? why, we were brought up together. Her mother is dead; she suckled both her and me.'

'If they bring you before the king, fear not.'

He came before the king.

'This girl, do you know her, my lad?'

'I do, we grew up together.'

'Will you bring her here?'

'I will. Build me a gilded galleon; give me twenty musicians; let me take your son with me; and let no one gainsay whatever I do. Then I will go. I shall take seven years to go and come.'

They took their bread, their water for seven years; they set out. They went to the maiden's country. At break of day Baldpate brought the galleon near the maiden's house; the maiden's house was close to the sea. Baldpate said, 'I'll go upon deck for a turn; don't any of you show yourselves.' He went up; he paced the deck.

The dervish's daughter arose from her sleep. The sun struck on the galleon; it struck, too, on the house. The girl went out, rubs her eyes. A man pacing up and down. She bowed forward and saw our Baldpate. She knew him: 'What wants he here?'

'What seek you here?'

'I've come for you, come to see you; it is so many years since I've seen you. Come aboard. Your father, where's he gone to?'

'Don't you know that my father has been painting my portrait? He's gone to sell it; I'm expecting him these last few days.'

'Come here, and let's have a little talk.'

The girl went to dress. Baldpate went to his crew. Hide yourselves; don't let a soul be seen; but the moment I get her into the cabin, do you cut the ropes; I shall be talking with her.'

She came into the cabin; they seated themselves; they talk; the galleon gets under weigh. He privily brought in the king's son.

Three Birds perched on the galleon

'Who is this?' said the girl. 'I am off.'

'Are you daft, my sister? Let's have some sweetmeats.' He gave her some; they intoxicated the girl.

'A little music to play to you,' said Baldpate.

He went, brought the musicians; they began to play. The girl said, 'I'm up, I'm off; my father's coming.'

'Sit down a bit, and let them play to you.' They play their music; she hears not the departure of the galleon.

'I'm off,' said the girl to Baldpate.

She went on deck and saw where her home was. 'Ah! my brother, what have you done to me?'

'Done to you! he who sits by you is the son of the king, and I'm come to fetch you for him.'

She wept and said, 'What shall I do? shall I fling myself into the sea?' No, she went and sat down by the king's son. Plenty of music and victuals and drink. Baldpate is sitting up aloft by himself; he is captain. They eat, they drink; he stirred not from his post.

Two or three days remained ere they landed. At break of dawn three birds perched on the galleon; no one was near him. The birds began talking: 'O bird, O bird, what is it, O bird? The dervish's daughter eats, drinks with the son of the king; she knows not what will befall them.'

'What will?' the other birds asked.

'As soon as he arrives, a little boat will come to take them off. The boat will upset, and the dervish's daughter and the king's son will be drowned; and whoever hears it and tells will be turned into stone to his knees.'

Baldpate listens; he is alone.

Early next morning the birds came back again. They began talking together: 'O bird, O bird, what is it, O bird? The dervish's daughter and the king's son eat, drink; they know not what will befall them. As soon as they land, as soon as they enter the gate, the gate will tumble down, it will crush them and kill them; and whoever hears it and tells will be turned into stone to the back.'

Day broke; the birds came back. 'O bird, O bird, what is it, O bird? The dervish's daughter eats, drinks; she knows not what will befall her.'

'What will?' the other birds asked.

'The marriage night a seven-headed dragon will come forth, and he will devour the king's son and the dervish's daughter; and whoever hears it and tells them will be turned into stone to the head.'

Baldpate says, all to himself, 'I shan't let any boats come.' He arose; he came opposite the palace; some boats came to take off the maiden.

'I want no boats.' Instead he spread his sails. The galleon backed, the galleon went ahead. One and all looked: 'Why, he will strand the galleon!'

'Let him be,' said the king, 'let him strand her.'

He stranded the galleon.

Baldpate said to the king, 'When I started to fetch this girl, did I not tell you you must let me do as I would? No one must interfere.'

He took the girl and the prince; he came to the gate. 'Pull it down.'

'Pull it down, why?' they asked.

'Did I not tell you no one must interfere?'

They set to and pulled it down. They went up, sat down, ate, drank, laugh, and talk.

The worm gnaws Baldpate within.

Night fell; they will bed the pair. Baldpate said; 'Where you sleep I also will sleep there.'

'The bridegroom and bride will sleep there; you can't.'

'What's our bargain?'

'Thou knowest.'

They went, they lay down; Baldpate took his sword, he lay down, he covered his head. At midnight he hears a dragon coming. He draws his sword; he cuts off its heads; he puts them beneath his pillow. The king's son awoke, and sees his sword in his hands. He cried, 'Baldpate will kill us.'

The father came and asked, 'What made you call out, my son?'

'Baldpate will kill us,' he answered.

They took and bound Baldpate's arms.

Day broke; the king summoned him. 'Why have you acted thus? Seven years you have gone, you have journeyed, and brought the maiden; and now you have risen to slay them.'

'What could I do?'

'You would kill my son, then will I kill you.'

'Thou knowest.'

They bind his arms, they lead him to cut off his head. As he went, Baldpate said to himself; 'They will cut off my head. If I tell, I shall be turned into stone. Come, bring me to the king; I have a couple of words to say to him.'

They brought him to the king.

'Why have you brought him here?'

'He has a couple of words to say to you.'

'Say them, my lad.'

'I, when I went to fetch the dervish's daughter, I was sitting alone on the galleon; your son was eating, drinking with the maiden. One morning three birds came; they began talking: "O bird, O bird, what is it, O bird? The dervish's daughter eats, drinks with the son of the king; she knows not what will befall her. And whoever hears it and tells will be turned into stone to his knees." No one but I was there; I heard it.'

As soon as Baldpate had said it, he was turned into stone to his knees. The king, seeing he was turned into stone, said, 'Prithee, my lad, say no more.'

'But I will,' Baldpate answered, and went on to tell of the gate; he was turned into stone to his back.

'The third time the birds came and talked together again, and I heard (that was why I wished to sleep with them): "A seven-headed dragon will come forth; he will devour them." And if you believe it not, look under the pillow.'

They went there; they saw the heads.

'It was I who killed him. Your son saw the sword in my hands, and he thought I would kill them. I could not tell him the truth.'

He was turned into stone to his head, They made a tomb for him.

The king's son arose; he took the road; he departed. 'Seven years has he wandered for me, I am going to wander seven years for him.'

The king's son went walking, walking. In a certain place there was water; he drank of it; he lay down. Baldpate came to him in a dream: 'Take a little earth from here, and go and sprinkle it on the tomb. He will rise from the stone.'

The king's son slept and slept. He arose; he takes some of the earth; he went to the tomb; he sprinkled the earth on it. Baldpate arose. 'How sound I've been sleeping!' he said.

'Seven years hast thou wandered for me, and seven years I have wandered for thee.'

He takes him, he brings him to the palace, he makes him a great one.

No. 3.--The Riddle

In those days there was a rich man. He had an only son, and the mother and the father loved him dearly., He went to school; all that there is in the world, he learned it. One day he arose; took four, five purses of money. Here, there he squandered it. Early next morning he arose again and went to his father. 'Give me more money.' He got more money, arose, went; by night he had spent it. Little by little he spent all the money.

And early once more he arose, and says to his father and mother, 'I want some money.'

'My child, there is no money left. Would you like the stew-pans? take them, go, sell them, and eat.'

He took and sold them: in a day or two he had spent it.

'I want some money.'

My son, we have no money. Take the clothes, go, sell them.'

In a day or two he had spent that money. He arose, and went to his father, 'I want some money.'

'My son, there is no money left us. If you like, sell the house.'

The lad took and sold the house. In a month he had spent the money; no money remained. 'Father I want some money.'

'My son, no riches remain to us, no house remains to us. If you like, take us to the slave-market, sell us.'

The lad took and sold them. His mother and his father said, 'Come this way, that we may see you.' The king bought the mother and father.

With the money for his mother the lad bought himself clothes, and with the money for his father got a horse.

One day, two days the father, the mother looked for the son that comes not; they fell a-weeping. The king's servants saw them weeping; they went, told it to the king. 'Those whom you bought weep loudly.'

'Call them to me.' The king called them. 'Why are you weeping.'

'We had a son; for him it is we weep.'

'Who are you, then? ' asked the king.

'We were not thus, my king; we had a son. He sold us, and we were weeping at his not coming to see us.'

Just as they were talking with the king, the lad arrived. The king set-to, wrote a letter, gave it him into his hand. 'Carry this letter to such and such a place.' In it the king wrote, 'The lad bearing this letter, cut his throat the minute you get it.'

The lad put on his new clothes, mounted his horse, put the letter in his bosom, took the road. He rode a long way; he was dying of thirst; and he sees a well. 'How am I to get water to drink? I will fasten this letter, and lower it into the well, and moisten my mouth a bit.' He lowered it, drew it up, squeezed it into his mouth.

'Let's see what this letter contains.'

See what it contains--'The minute he delivers the letter, cut his throat.' The lad stood there fair mesmerised.

In a certain place there was a king's daughter. They go to propound a riddle to her. If she guesses it, she will cut off his head; and if she cannot, he will marry the maiden.

The lad arose, went to the king's palace.

'What are you come for, my lad?'

'I would speak with the king's daughter.'

'Speak with her you shall. If she guesses your riddle, she will cut off your head; and if she cannot, you will get the maiden.'

'That's what I'm come for.'

He sat down in front of the maiden. The maiden said, 'Tell your riddle.'

He lowered the letter into the well

The lad said, 'My mother I wore her, my father I rode him, from my death I drank water.'

The maiden looked in her book, could not find it. 'Grant me a three days' respite.'

'I grant it you,' said the lad. The lad arose, went to an inn, goes to sleep there.

The maiden saw she cannot find it out. The maiden set-to, had an underground passage made to the place where the lad lies sleeping. At midnight the maid arose, went to him, took the lad in her arms.

'I am thine, thou art mine, only tell me the riddle.'

'Not likely I should tell you. Strip yourself,' said the lad to the maiden. The maiden stripped herself.

'Tell me it.' Then he told her.

The maiden clapped her hands; her servants came, took the maiden, and let her go. The maiden was wearing the lad's sark, and the lad was wearing the maiden's.

Day broke. They summoned the lad. The lad mounted his horse, and rides to the palace. The people see the lad. ''Tis a pity; they'll kill him.'

He went up, and stood face to face with the king.

'My daughter has guessed your riddle,' said the king.

'How did she guess it, my king? At night when I was asleep, there came a bird to my breast. I caught it, I killed it, I cooked it. Just as I was going to eat it, it flew away.'

The king says, 'Kill him; he's wandering.'

'I am not wandering, my king. I told your daughter the riddle. Your daughter had an underground passage made, and she came to where I was sleeping, came to my arms. I caught her, I stripped her, I took her to my bosom, I told her the riddle. She clapped her hands; her servants came and took her. And if you don't believe, I am wearing her sark, and she is wearing mine.'

The king saw it was true.

Forty days, forty nights they made a marriage. He took the maiden, went, bought back his father, his mother.

NO. 4.--STORY OF THE BRIDGE

In olden days there were twelve brothers. And the eldest brother, the carpenter Manoli, was making the long bridge. One side he makes; one side falls. The twelve brothers had one mistress, and they all had to do with her. They called her to them, 'Dear bride.' On her head was the tray; in her hands was a child. Whoseso wife came first, she will come to the twelve brothers. Manoli's wife, Lénga, will come to the twelve brothers. Said his wife, 'Thou hast not eaten bread with me. What has befallen thee that thou eatest not bread with me? My ring has fallen into the water. Go and fetch my ring.' Her husband said, 'I will fetch thy ring out of the water.' Up to his two breasts came the water in the depth of the bridge there. He came into the fountain, he was drowned. Beneath he became a talisman, the innermost foundation of the bridge. Manoli's eyes became the great open arch of the bridge. 'God send a wind to blow, that the tray may fall from the head of her who bears it in front of Lénga.' A snake crept out before Lénga, and she feared, and said, 'Now have I fear at sight of the snake, and am sick. Now is it not bad for my children?' Another man seized her, and sought to drown her, Manoli's wife. She said, 'Drown me not in the water. I have little children.' She bowed herself over the sea, where the carpenter Manoli made the bridge. Another man called Manoli's wife; with him she went on the road. There, when they went on the road, he went to the tavern, he was weary; the man went, drank the juice of the grape, got drunk. Before getting home, he killed Manoli's wife, Lénga.

CHAPTER II

ROUMANIAN GYPSY STORIES

The Vampire

No. 5.--The Vampire

THERE was an old woman in a village. And grown-up maidens met and span, and made a 'bee.' And the young sparks came and laid hold of the girls, and pulled them about and kissed them. But one girl had no sweetheart to lay hold of her and kiss her. And she was a strapping lass, the daughter of wealthy peasants; but three whole days no one came near her. And she looked at the big girls, her comrades. And no one troubled himself with her. Yet she was a pretty girl, a prettier was not to be found. Then came a fine young spark, and took her in his arms and kissed her, and stayed with her until cock-crow. And when the cock crowed at dawn he departed. The old woman saw he had cock's feet. And she kept looking at the lad's feet, and she said, 'Nita, my lass, did you see anything?'

'I didn't notice.'

'Then didn't I see he had cock's feet?'

'Let be, mother, I didn't see it.'

And the girl went home and slept; and she arose and went off to the spinning, where many more girls were holding a 'bee.' And the young sparks came, and took each one his sweetheart. And they kissed them, and stayed a while, and went home. And the girl's handsome young spark came and took her in his arms and kissed her and pulled her about, and stayed with her till midnight. And the cock began to crow. The young spark heard the cock crowing, and departed. What said the old woman who was in the hut, 'Nita, did you notice that he had horse's hoofs?'

'And if he had, I didn't see.'

Then the girl departed to her home. And she slept and arose in the morning, and did her work that she had to do. And night came, and she took her spindle and went to the old woman in the hut. And the other girls came, and the young sparks came, and each laid hold of his sweetheart. But the pretty girl looks at them. Then the young sparks gave over and departed home. And only the girl remained neither a long time nor a short time. Then came the girl's young spark. Then what will the girl do? She took heed, and stuck a needle and thread in his back. And he departed when the cock crew, and she knew not where he had gone to. Then the girl arose in the morning and took the thread, and followed up the thread, and saw him in a grave where he was sitting. Then the girl trembled and went back home. At night the young spark that was in the grave came to the old woman's house and saw that the girl was not there. He asked the old woman, 'Where's Nita?'

'She has not come.'

Then he went to Nita's house, where she lived, and called, 'Nita, are you at home?'

Nita answered, 'I am'.

'Tell me what you saw when you came to the church. For if you don't tell me I will kill your father.'

'I didn't see anything.'

Then he looked, and he killed her father, and departed to his grave.

Next night he came back. 'Nita, tell me what you saw.' I didn't see anything.'

'Tell me, or I will kill your mother, as I killed your father. Tell me what you saw.'

'I didn't see anything.'

Then he killed her mother, and departed to his grave. Then the girl arose in the morning. And she had twelve servants. And she said to them, 'See, I have much money and many oxen and many sheep; and they shall come to the twelve of you as a gift, for I shall die to-night. And it will fare ill with you if you bury me not in the forest at the foot of an apple-tree.'

At night came the young spark from the grave and asked, Nita, are you at home?'

'I am.'

'Tell me, Nita, what you saw three days ago, or I will kill you, as I killed your parents.'

'I have nothing to tell you.'

Then he took and killed her. Then, casting a look, he departed to his grave.

So the servants, when they arose in the morning, found Nita dead. The servants took her and laid her out decently. They sat and made a hole in the wall and passed her through the hole, and carried her, as she had bidden, and buried her in the forest by the apple-tree.

And half a year passed by, and a prince went to go and course hares with greyhounds and other dogs. And he went to hunt, and the hounds ranged the forest and came to the maiden's grave. And a flower grew out of it, the like of which for beauty there was not in the whole kingdom. So the hounds came on her monument, where she was buried, and they began to bark and scratched at the maiden's grave. Then the prince took and called the dogs with his horn, and the dogs came not. The prince said, 'Go quickly thither.'

Four huntsmen arose and came and saw the flower burning like a candle. They returned to the prince, and he asked them, 'What is it?'

'It is a flower, the like was never seen.'

Then the lad heard, and came to the maiden's grave, and saw the flower and plucked it. And he came home and showed it to his father and mother. Then he took and put it in a vase at his bed-head where he slept. Then the flower arose from the vase and turned a somersault, and became a full-grown maiden. And she took the lad and kissed him, and bit him and pulled him about, and slept with him in her arms, and put her hand under his head. And he knew it not. When the dawn came she became a flower again.

In the morning the lad rose up sick, and complained to his father and mother, 'Mammy, my shoulders hurt me, and my head hurts me.'

His mother went and brought a wise woman and tended him. He asked for something to eat and drink. And he waited a bit, and then went to his business that he had to do. And he went home again at night. And he ate and drank and lay down on his couch, and sleep seized him. Then the flower arose and again became a full-grown maiden. And she took him again in her arms, and slept with him, and sat with him in her arms. And he slept. And she went back to the vase. And he arose, and his bones hurt him, and he told his mother and his father. Then his father said to his wife, 'It began with the coming of the flower. Something must be the matter, for the boy is quite ill. Let us watch to-night, and post ourselves on one side, and see who comes to our son.'

Night came, and the prince laid himself in his bed to sleep. Then the maiden arose from the vase, and became there was never anything more fair--as burns the flame of a candle. And his mother and his father, the king, saw the maiden, and laid hands on her. Then the prince arose out of his sleep, and saw the maiden that she was fair. Then he took her in his arms and kissed her, and lay down in his bed, slept till day.

And they made a marriage and ate and drank. The folk marvelled, for a being so fair as that maiden was not to be found in all the realm. And he dwelt with her half a year, and she bore a golden boy, two apples in his hand. And it pleased the prince well.

Then her old sweetheart heard it, the vampire who had made love to her, and had killed her. He arose and came to her and asked her, 'Nita, tell me, what did you see me doing?'

'I didn't see anything.'

'Tell me truly, or I will kill your child, your little boy, as I killed your father and mother. Tell me truly.'

'I have nothing to tell you.'

And he killed her boy. And she arose and carried him to the church and buried him.

At night the vampire came again and asked her, 'Tell me, Nita, what you saw.'

'I didn't see anything.'

'Tell me, or I will kill the lord whom you have wedded.'

Then Nita arose and said, 'It shall not happen that you kill my lord. God send you burst.'

The vampire heard what Nita said, and burst. Ay, he died, and burst for very rage. In the morning Nita arose and saw the floor swimming two hand's-breadth deep in blood. Then Nita bade her father-in-law take out the vampire's heart with all speed. Her father-in-law, the king, hearkened, and opened him and took out his heart, and gave it into Nita's hand. And she went to the grave of her boy and dug the boy up, applied the heart, and the boy arose. And Nita went to her father and to her mother, and anointed them with the blood, and they arose. Then, looking on them, Nita told all the troubles she had borne, and what she had suffered at the hands of the vampire.

No. 6.--God's Godson

There was a queen. From youth to old age that queen never bore but one son. That son was a hero. So soon as he was born, he said to his father, 'Father, have you no sword or club?'

'No, my child, but I will order one to be made for you.'

The son said, 'Don't order one, father: I will go just as I am.'

So the son took and departed, and journeyed a long while, and took no heed, till he came into a great forest. So in that forest he stretched himself beneath a tree to rest a bit, for he was weary. And he sat there a while. Then the holy God and St. Peter came on the lad; and he was unbaptized. So the holy God asked him, 'Where are you going, my lad?'

'I am going in quest of heroic achievements, old fellow.'

Then the holy God thought and thought, and made a church. And he caused sleep to fall on that lad, and bade St. Peter lift him, and went with him to the church, and gave him the name Handak. And the holy God said to him, 'Godson, a hero like you there shall never be any other; and do you take my god-daughter.'

For there was a maiden equally heroic, and equally baptized by God. And she was his god-daughter, and he told his godson to take her. And he gave him a wand of good fortune and a sword. And he endowed him with strength, and set him down. And his godfather departed to heaven, like the holy God that he was.

And Handak perceived that God had endowed him with strength, and he set out in quest of heroic achievements, and journeyed a long while, and took no heed. So he came into a great forest. And there was a dragon three hundred years old. And his eyelashes reached down to the ground, and likewise his hair. And the lad went to him and said, 'All hail.'

'You are welcome.'

Soon as that hero [the dragon] heard his voice, he knew that it was God's godson.

And the lad, Handak, asked him, 'Does God's god-daughter dwell far hence?'

'She dwells not far; it is but a three days' journey.'

And the lad took and departed, and journeyed three days until he came to the maiden's. Soon as the maiden saw him, she recognised him for her godfather's godson. And she let him into her house, and served up food to him, and ate with him and asked him, 'What seek you here, Handak?'

He said, 'I have come on purpose to marry you.'

'With whom?'

'With myself an you will.'

She said, 'I will not have it so without a fight.'

And the lad said, 'Come let us fight.'

And they fell to fighting, and fought three days; and the lad vanquished her. And he took her, and went to their godfather. And he crowned them and made a marriage. And they became rulers over all lands. And I came away, and told the story.

No. 7.--The Snake who became the King's Son-in-law

There were an old man and an old woman. From their youth up to their old age they had never had any children (lit. 'made any children of their bones'). So the old woman was always scolding with the old man--what can they do, for there they are old, old people? The old woman said, 'Who will look after us when we grow older still?'

'Well, what am I to do, old woman?'

'Go you, old man, and find a son for us.'

So the old man arose in the morning, and took his axe in his hand, and departed and journeyed till mid-day, and came into a forest, and sought three days and found nothing. Then the old man could do no more for hunger. He set out to return home. So as he was coming back, he found a little snake and put it in a handkerchief, and carried it home. And he brought up the snake on sweet milk. The snake grew a week and two days, and he put it in a jar. The time came when the snake grew as big as the jar. The snake talked with his father, 'My time has come to marry me. Go, father, to the king, and ask his daughter for me.'

When the old man heard that the snake wants the king's daughter, he smote himself with his hands. 'Woe is me, darling! How can I go to the king? For the king will kill me.'

The snake who became the King's God-son

What said he? 'Go, father, and fear not. For what he wants of you, that will I give him.'

The old man went to the king. 'All hail, O king!'

'Thank you, old man.'

'King, I am come to form an alliance by marriage.'

'An alliance by marriage!' said the king. 'You are a peasant, and I am a king.'

'That matters not, O king. If you will give me your daughter, I will give you whatever you want.'

What said the king? 'Old man, if that be so, see this great forest. Fell it all, and make it a level field; and plough it for me, and break up all the earth; and sow it with millet by to-morrow. And mark well what I tell you: you must bring me a cake made with sweet milk. Then will I give you the maiden.'

Said the old man, 'All right, O king.'

The old man went weeping to the snake. When the snake saw his father weeping he said, 'Why weepest thou, father?'

'How should I not weep, darling? For see what the king said, that I must fell this great forest, and sow millet; and it must grow up by to-morrow, and be ripe. And I must make a cake with sweet milk and give it him. Then he will give me his daughter.'

What said the snake? 'Father, don't fear for that, for I will do what you have told me.'

The old man: 'All right, darling, if you can manage it.'

The old man went off to bed.

What did the snake? He arose and made the forest a level plain, and sowed millet, and thought and thought, and it was grown up by daybreak. When the old man got up, he finds a sack of millet, and he made a cake with sweet milk. The old man took the cake and went to the king.

'Here, O king, I have done your bidding.'

When the king saw that, he marvelled. 'My old fellow, hearken to me. I have one thing more for you to do. Make me a golden bridge from my palace to your house, and let golden apple-trees and pear-trees grow on the side of this bridge. Then will I give you my daughter.'

When the old man heard that, he began to weep, and went home.

What said the snake? 'Why weepest thou, father?'

The old man said, 'I am weeping, darling, for the miseries which God sends me. The king wants a golden bridge from his palace to our house, and apple and pear-trees on the side of this bridge.'

The snake said, 'Fear not, father, for I will do as the king said.' Then the snake thought and thought, and the golden bridge was made as the king had said. The snake did that in the night-time. The king arose at midnight; he thought the sun was at meat [*i.e.* it was noon]. He scolded the servants for not having called him in the morning.

The servants said, 'King, it is night, not day'; and, seeing that, the king marvelled.

In the morning the old man came. 'Good-day, father-in-law.'

'Thank you, father-in-law. Go, father-in-law, and bring your son, that we may hold the wedding.'

He, when he went, said, 'Hearken, what says the king? You are to go there for the king to see you.'

What said the snake? 'My father, if that be so, fetch the cart, and put in the horses, and I will get into it to go to the king.'

No sooner said, no sooner done. He got into the cart and drove to the king. When the king saw him, he trembled with all his lords. One lord older than the rest, said, 'Fly not, O king, it were not well of you. For he did what you told him; and shall not you do what you promised? He will kill us all. Give him your daughter, and hold the marriage as you promised.'

What said the king? 'My old man, here is the maiden whom you demand. Take her to you.'

And he gave him also a house by itself for her to live in with her husband. She, the bride, trembled at him.

The snake said, 'Fear not, my wife, for I am no snake as you see me. Behold me as I am.'

He turned a somersault, and became a golden youth, in armour clad; he had but to wish to get anything. The maiden, when she saw that, took him in her arms and kissed him, and said, 'Live, my king, many years. I thought you would eat me.'

The king sent a man to see how it fares with his daughter. When the king's servant came, what does he see? The maiden fairer, lovelier than before. He went back to the king. 'O king, your daughter is safe and sound.'

'As God wills with her,' said the king. Then he called many people and held the marriage; and they kept it up three days and three nights, and the marriage was consummated. And I came away and told the story.

No. 8.--The Bad Mother

There was an emperor. He had been married ten years, but had no children. And God granted that his empress conceived and bore a son. Now that son was heroic; there was none other found like him. And the father lived half a year longer, and died. Then what is the lad to do? He took and departed in quest of heroic achievements. And he journeyed a long while, and took no heed, and came into a great forest. In that forest there was a certain house, and in that house were twelve dragons. Then the lad went straight thither, and saw that there was no one. He opened the door and went in, and he saw a sabre on a nail and took it, and posted himself behind the door, and waited for the coming of the dragons. They, when they came, did not go in all at once, but went in one by one. The lad waited, sabre in hand; and as each one went in, he cut off his head, flung it on the floor. So the lad killed eleven dragons, and the youngest dragon remained. And the lad went out to him, and took and fought with him, and fought half a day. And the lad vanquished the dragon, and took him and put him in a jar, and fastened it securely.

And the lad went to walk, and came on another house, where there was only a maiden. And when he saw the maiden, how did she please his heart. As for the maiden, the lad pleased her just as well. And the maiden was yet more heroic than the lad. And they formed a strong love. And the lad told the maiden how he had killed eleven dragons, and one he had left alive and put in a jar.

The maiden said, 'You did ill not to kill it; but now let it be.'

And the lad said to the maiden, 'I will go and fetch my mother, for she is alone at home.'

Then the maiden said, 'Fetch her, but you will rue it. But go and fetch her, and dwell with her.'

So the lad departed to fetch his mother. He took his mother, and brought her into the house of the dragons whom he had slain. And he said to his mother, 'Go into every room; only into this chamber do not go.'

His mother said, 'I will not, darling.'

And the lad departed into the forest to hunt.

And his mother went into the room where he had told her not to go. And when she opened the door, the dragon saw her and said to her, 'Empress, give me a little water, and I will do you much good.'

She went and gave him water and he said to her, 'Dost love me, then will I take thee, and thou shalt be mine empress.'

'I love thee,' she said.

Then the dragon said to her, 'What will you do, to get rid of your son, that we may be left to ourselves? Make yourself ill, and say you have seen a dream, that he must bring you a porker of the sow in the other world; that, if he does not bring it you, you will die; but that, if he brings it you, you will recover.'

Then she went into the house, and tied up her head, and made herself ill. And when the lad came home and saw her head tied up, he asked her, 'What's the matter, mother?'

She said, 'I am ill, darling. I shall die. But I have seen a dream, to eat a porker of the sow in the other world.'

Then the lad began to weep, for his mother will die. And he took and departed. Then he went to his sweetheart, and told her. 'Maiden, my mother will die. And she has seen a dream, that I must bring her a porker from the other world.'

The maiden said, 'Go, and be prudent; and come to me as you return. Take my horse with the twelve wings, and mind the sow does not seize you, else she 'll eat both you and the horse.'

So the lad took the horse and departed. He came there, and when the sun was midway in his course he went to the little pigs, and took one, and fled. Then the sow heard him, and hurried after him to devour him. And at the very brink (of the other world), just as he was leaping out, the sow bit off half of the horse's tail. So the lad went to the maiden. And the maiden came out, and took the little pig, and hid it, and put another in its stead. Then he went home to his mother, and gave her that little pig, and she dressed it and ate, and said that she was well.

Take my horse with twelve wings

Three or four days later she made herself ill again, as the dragon had shown her.

When the lad came, he asked her, 'What's the matter now, mother?

'I am ill again, darling, and I have seen a dream that you must bring me an apple from the golden apple-tree in the other world.'

So the lad took and departed to the maiden; and when the maiden saw him so troubled, she asked him, 'What's the matter, lad?'

'What's the matter! my mother is ill again. And she has seen a dream that I am to bring her an apple from the apple-tree in the other world.'

Then the maiden knew that his mother was compassing his destruction (lit. 'was walking to eat his head'), and she said to the lad, 'Take my horse and go, but be careful the apple-tree does not seize you there. Come to me, as you return.'

And the lad took and departed, and came to the brink of the world. And he let himself in, and went to the apple-tree at mid-day when the apples were resting. And he took an apple and ran away. Then the leaves perceived it and began to scream; and the apple-tree took itself after him to lay its hand on him and kill him. And the lad came out from the brink, and arrived in our world, and went to the maiden. Then the maiden took the apple, stole it from him, and hid it, and put another in its stead. And the lad stayed a little longer with her, and departed to his mother. Then his mother, when she saw him, asked him, 'Have you brought it, darling?'

'I've brought it, mother.'

So she took the apple and ate, and said there was nothing more the matter with her.

In a week's time the dragon told her to make herself ill again, and to ask for water from the great mountains. So she made herself ill.

When the lad saw her ill, he began to weep and said, 'My mother will die, God. She's always ill.' Then he went to her and asked her, 'What's the matter, mother?'

'I am like to die, darling. But I shall recover if you will bring me water from the great mountains.'

Then the lad tarried no longer. He went to the maiden and said to her, 'My mother is ill again; and she has seen a dream that I must fetch her water from the great mountains.'

The maiden said, 'Go, lad; but I fear the clouds will catch you, and the mountains there, and will kill you. But do you take my horse with twenty-and-four wings; and when you get there, wait afar off till mid-day, for at mid-day the mountains and the clouds set themselves at table and eat. Then do you go with the pitcher, and draw water quickly, and fly.'

Then the lad took the pitcher, and departed thither to the mountains, and waited till the sun had reached the middle of his course. And he went and drew water and fled. And the clouds and the mountains perceived him, and took themselves after him, but they could not catch him. And the lad came to the maiden. Then the maiden went and took the pitcher with the water, and put another in its stead without his knowing it. And the lad arose and went home, and gave water to his mother, and she recovered.

Then the lad departed into the forest to hunt. His mother went to the dragon and told him, 'He has brought me the water. What am I to do now with him?'

'What are you to do! why, take and play cards with him. You must say, "For a wager, as I used to play with your father."'

So the lad came home and found his mother merry: it pleased him well. And she said to him at table, as they were eating, 'Darling, when your father was alive, what did we do? When we had eaten and risen up, we took and played cards for a wager.'

Then the lad: 'If you like, play with me, mother.'

So they took and played cards; and his mother beat him. And she took silken cords, and bound his two hands so tight that the cord cut into his hands.

And the lad began to weep, and said to his mother, 'Mother, release me or I die.'

She said, 'That is just what I was wanting to do to you.' And she called the dragon, 'Come forth, dragon, come and kill him.'

Then the dragon came forth, and took him, and cut him in pieces, and put him in the saddle-bags, and placed him on his horse, and let him go, and said to the horse, 'Carry him, horse, dead, whence thou didst carry him alive.'

Then the horse hurried to the lad's sweetheart, and went straight to her there. Then, when the maiden saw him, she began to weep, and she took him and put piece to piece; where one was missing, she cut the porker, and supplied flesh from the porker. So she put all the pieces of him in their place. And she took the water and poured it on him, and he became whole. And she squeezed the apple in his mouth, and brought him to life.

So when the lad arose, he went home to his mother, and drove a stake into the earth, and placed both her and the dragon on one great pile of straw. And he set it alight, and they were consumed. And he departed thence, and took the maiden, and made a marriage, and kept up the marriage three months day and night. And I came away and told the story.

No. 9.--The Mother's Chastisement

There was an emperor's son, and he went to hunt. And he departed from the hunters by himself. And by a certain stack there was a maiden. He passed near the stack, and heard her lamenting. He took that maiden, and brought her home.

'See, mother, what I've found.'

His mother took her to the kitchen to the cook to bring her up. She brought her up twelve years. The empress dressed her nicely, and put her in the palace to lay the table. The prince loved her, for she was so fair that in all the world there was none so fair as she. The prince loved her three years, and the empress knew it not.

Once he said, 'I will take a wife, mother.'

'From what imperial family?'

'I wish to marry her who lays the table.'

'Not her, mother's darling!'

'If I don't take her, I shall die.'

'Take her.'

He left her big with child

And he took her; he married her. And an order came for him to go to battle. He left her big with child.

The empress called two servants. 'Take her into the forest and kill her, and bring me her heart and little finger.'

They put her in the carriage, and drove her into the forest; after them ran a whelp. And they brought her into the forest, and were going to kill her, and she said, 'Kill me not, for I have used you well.'

'How are we to take her the heart, then?'

'Kill the whelp, for its heart is just like a human one, and cut off my little finger.'

They killed the whelp, and cut off her little finger, and took out the whelp's heart.

And she cried, 'Gather wood for me, and make me a fire; and strip off bark for me, and build me a hut.'

They built her a hut, and made her a fire, and went away home, bringing the heart and the little finger.

She brought forth a son. God and St. Peter came and baptized him; and God gave him a gun that he should become a hunter. Whatever he saw he would kill with the gun. And God gave him the name Silvester. And God made a house of the hut, and the fire no longer died. And God gave them a certain loaf; they were always eating, and it was never finished.

The boy grew big, and he took his gun in his hand, and went into the forest. And what he saw he killed, carried to his mother, and they ate. Walking in the *forest,* he came upon the *dragons' palace,* and sat before the door. At mid-day the dragons were coming home. He saw them from afar, eleven (*sic*) in number; and *eleven* he shot with his gun, and *one* he merely stunned. And he took them, and carried them into the palace, and shut them up in a room; and he went to *his mother,* and said, 'Come with me, mother.'

'Where am I to go to, mother's darling?'

'Come with me, where I take you to.'

He went with her to the palace. 'Take to thee, mother, twelve keys. *Go into any room you choose, but into this room do not go.*'

He *went into the forest to hunt.*

She said, 'Why did my son tell me not to go in here? But I will go to see what is there.'

She opened the door.

The dragon asked her, 'If thou art a virgin, be my sister; but if thou art a wife, be my wife.'

'I am a wife.'

'Then be my wife.'

'I will; but will you do the right thing by me?'

'I will.'

'Swear, then.'

I swear.'

The dragon swore. The dragon said to her, 'Swear also thou.'

She also swore. They kissed one another on the mouth. She brought him to her into the house; they drank and ate, and loved one another.

Her son came from the forest. She saw him. She said, 'My son is coming; go back into the room.'

He went back, and she shut him in.

In the morning her son went again into the forest to hunt. She admitted the dragon again to her. They drank and ate. He said to her, 'How shall we kill your son? Then we'll live finely. *Make yourself ill, and say that you have seen a dream, that he must bring* milk from the she-bear for you to drink. Then you'll have nothing to trouble you, for the she-bear will devour him.'

He came home from the forest. '*What's the matter with you, mother?*'

'*I shall die, but I saw a dream.* Bring me milk from the she-bear.'

'I'll bring it you, mother.'

He went into the forest, and found the she-bear. He was going to shoot her.

She cried, 'Stop, man. What do you want?'

'You to give me milk.'

She said, 'I will give it you. Have you a pail?'

'I have.'

'Come and milk.'

He milked her, and brought it to his mother.

'Here, mother.'

She pretended to drink, but poured it forth.

In the morning he went again into the forest, and met the Moon. 'Who art thou?'

'I am the Moon.'

'Be a sister to me.'

'But who art thou?'

'I am Silvester.'

'Then thou art God's godson, for God takes care of thee. I also am God's.'

'Be a sister to me.'

'I will be a sister to thee.'

He went further; he met Friday. 'Who art thou?'

'I am Friday, but who art thou?'

'I am Silvester.'

'Thou art God's godson; I also am God's.'

'Be a sister to me.'

He went home. His mother saw him. 'My son is coming.'

'Send him to the wild *sow* to bring thee milk, for she will *devour* him.'

'Always sick, mother?'

'I am. I have seen a dream. Bring me milk from the wild sow.'

I know not whether or no I shall bring it, but I will try.'

He went; he found the sow; he was going to shoot her with his gun. She cried, 'Don't, don't shoot me. What do you want?'

'Give me milk.'

'Have you a pail? come and milk.'

He brought it to his mother. She pretended to drink, but poured it forth. He went again into the forest.

She admitted the dragon to her. 'In vain, for the sow has not devoured him.'

'Then send him to the *Mountains* of Blood, that butt at one another like rams, to bring thee water, the water of life and the water of healing. If he does not die there, he never will.'

'I have seen a dream, that you bring me water from the Mountains of Blood, which butt at one another like rams, for then there will be nothing the matter with me.'

He went to the Moon.

'Whither away, brother?'

'I am going to the mountains to fetch water for my mother.'

'Don't go, brother; you will die there.'

'Bah! I will go there.'

'*Take thee my horse* when thou goest, for my horse will carry thee thither. And take thee a watch, for they butt at one another from morning till noon, and at *noon* they rest for two hours. So when you come there at the twelfth hour, draw water in two pails from the two wells.'

He came thither at mid-day, and dismounted, and drew water in two pails, the water of life and the water of healing. And he came back to the Moon; and the Moon said, 'Lie down and sleep, and rest, for you are worn out.'

She hid that water, and *poured in other.*

He arose. 'Come, sister, I will depart home.'

'Take my horse, and go riding. Take the saddle-bags.'

He went home to his mother. His mother saw him coming on horseback, and said to the dragon, 'My son is coming on horseback.'

Tell him that you have seen a dream, that you bind his fingers behind his back with a *silken cord;* and that if he can burst it he will become a hero, and you will grow strong.'

'Bind away, mother.'

She made a thick silken cord, and bound his fingers behind his back. He tugged, and grew red in the face; he tugged again, he grew blue; he tugged the third time, he grew black.

And she cried, 'Come, dragon, and cut his throat.'

The dragon came to him. 'Well, what shall I do to you now?'

'Cut me all in bits, and put me in the saddle-bags, and place me on my horse. Thither, whence he carried me living, let him carry me dead.'

He *cut him in pieces, put him in the saddle-bags, and placed him on the horse*. 'Go, *whence thou didst carry him living, carry him dead.*'

The horse went straight to the Moon. The Moon came out, and saw him, and took him in, and called Wednesday, and called Friday; and they laid him in a big trough, and washed him bravely, and placed him on a table, and put him all together, *bit by bit*; and they *took the water* of healing, and sprinkled him, and *he became whole*; and they took the water of life, and sprinkled him, and he came *to life*.

'Ah! I was sleeping soundly.'

'You would have slept for ever if I had not come.'

'I will go, sister, to my mother.'

'Go not, brother.'

'Bah! I will.'

'Well, go, and God be with thee. Take thee my sword.'

He went to his mother. His mother was singing and dancing with the dragon. He went in to the dragon. 'Good day to you both.'

'Thanks.'

'Come, what shall I do to you, dragon?'

'Cut me in little pieces, and put me in the saddle-bags, and place me on my horse. Whence he carried me living, let him carry me also dead.'

He cut him in little pieces, put him in the saddle-bags, placed him on his horse, and dug out the horse's eyes. 'Go whither thou wilt.'

Away went the horse, and kept knocking his head against the trees; and the pieces of flesh kept falling from the saddle-bags. The crows kept eating the flesh.

Silvester shot a hare, and skinned it, and spitted it, and roasted it at the fire. And he said to his mother, 'Mother, look straight at me.'

His mother looked at him. He struck her in the eyes, and her eyes leapt out of her head. And he took her by the hand, led her to a jar, said to her, 'Mother, when thou hast filled this jar with tears, then God pardon thee; and when thou hast eaten a bundle of hay, and filled the jar with tears, then God pardon thee, and restore thee thine eyes.'

And he bound her there, and departed, and left her three years. In three years she came back to his recollection. 'I will go to my mother, and see what she is doing.'

Now she has filled the jar, and eaten the bundle of hay.

'Now may God pardon thee; now I also pardon thee. Depart, and God be with thee.'

No. 10.--The Three Princesses and the Unclean Spirit

There was a king; and from youth to old age he had no son. In his old age three daughters were born to him. And the very morning of their birth the Unclean Spirit came and took them, the three maidens. And he fought to win a woman, the Serpent-Maiden; and half his moustache turned white, and half all the hair on his head, for the sake of the Serpent-Maiden. Time passed by, and he had no son; and his daughters the Unclean Spirit had carried away.

Then he took and thought. 'What am I to do, wife? I will go for three years (*sic*); and, when I return, let me find a son born of you. If in a year's time I find not one, I will kill you.'

He went and journeyed a year and a day. His wife took and thought. As she was a-thinking, a man went by with apples: whoso eats one of his apples shall conceive. Then she went, and took an apple, and ate the apple, and she conceived. The time came that she should bring forth. And she brought forth a son, and called his name Cosmas. So her king came that night, and sent a messenger to ask his wife.

She said, 'Your bidding is fulfilled.'

Then he went in, and, when he saw the lad, his heart was full.

And the time came when the lad grew big, and he looked the very picture of his father. The time came that his father died. By that time he felt himself a man, and he put forth his little finger, and lifted the palace up. Then he came back from hunting, and he lifted the foundation of the palace, and told his mother to place her breast beneath it. Then his mother placed her breast beneath the foundation, and he left it pressing upon her. Then she cried aloud.

The lad said to her, 'Mother, tell me, why was my father's moustache half white?'

Then she said to him, 'Why, darling, your father fought nine years to win the Serpent-Maiden, and never won her.'

Then he asked, 'And have I no brother?'

'No,' she said; 'but you have three sisters, and the Unclean Spirit carried them away.'

And he asked, 'Whither did he carry them?'

Then she said he had carried them to the Land of the Setting Sun.

Then he took his father's saddle and his bridle and likewise his father's colt, and set out in quest of his sisters, and arrived at his sister's house, and hurled his mace, and smashed the plum-trees.

Then his sister came out and said to him, 'Why have you smashed the plum-trees? For the Unclean Spirit will come and kill you.'

Then he said, 'I would not have you think ill of me; but kindly come and give me a draught of wine and a morsel of bread.'

Then she brought bread and wine. As she was handing him the bread and wine, she noticed her father's colt, and recognised it. Then she said, 'This must be my father's horse.'

Take notice then that I also am his.'

Then she fell on his neck, and he on hers.

Then she said to him, 'My brother, the Unclean Spirit will come from the Twelfth Region. And he will come and destroy you.'

Then the Unclean Spirit came, and hurled his mace; and it opened twelve doors, and hung itself on its peg. Then Cosmas took it, and hurled it twelve regions away from him. Then the Unclean Spirit took it, and came home with it in his hand, and asked, 'Wife, I smell mortal man?'

(Meanwhile she had turned her brother into an ear-ring, and put him in her ear.)

Then she said, 'You're for ever eating corpses, and are meaning to eat me, too, for I also am mortal.'

And he set his bugle in his mouth

Then he said to her, 'Don't tell lies; my brother-in-law has come.'

'Well, then, and if your brother-in-law has come, will you eat him?'

Then he said, 'I will not.'

'Swear it on your sword that you will not eat him.'

Then she took him out of her ear, and set him at table. He ate at table with the Unclean Spirit.

Then the lad went outside, and creeps into the fetlock of his colt, and hid himself there. Then the Unclean Spirit arose, and hunted everywhere, and failed to light on him. And he set his bugle to his mouth, and blew a blast, and summoned all the birds upon the horse, and they searched every hair of the horse. And just as he was coming to the fetlock, then the cocks crowed, and he fell.

Cosmas came forth, and went to him. 'Good day, brother-in-law.'

Then he asked him, 'Where were you?'

'Why, I was in the hay, before the horse.'

Then Cosmas took leave of them, and went to his other sisters, and did with them just as with this one.

Then his little sister asked him, 'Where are you going, my brother?'

'I am going to tend the white mare, and get one of her colts, and I am going to win the Serpent-Maiden.'

Then she said to him, 'Go, my brother, and if you get the colt, come to me.'

He went.

Now some peasants were hunting a wolf to slay it. The wolf said, 'Cosmas, don't abandon me. Send the peasants the wrong way, that they may not kill me; and take one of my hairs, and put it in your pocket. And whenever you think of me, there I am, wherever you may be.'

Going further, he came on a crow that had broken its wing, and it said, 'Don't pass me by, Cosmas; bind my wing up; and I will give you a feather to put in your pocket, and whenever you are in any difficulty, I'll be with you.'

Going still further, he came on a fish, which said, 'Cosmas, don't pass me by. Tie me to your horse's tail, and put me in the water, for I will do you much good.'

He did so, and put it in the water.

Then he came to the old woman who owned the white mare; and she sat before her door; and he said to her, 'Will you give me a colt of the white mare, old one?'

The old wife said, 'If you can find her three days running, one of her colts is yours. But if you can't find her, I will cut off your head, and stick it on yonder stake.'

'I'll find her,' he said.

And she gave him the white mare, and away he went with her to try and find her. So the mare ran in among the sheep, and took and hid herself in the earth. And the lad arose and searched for the mare, and failed to light on her. And the wolf came into his mind; and he thought of him.

And the wolf came and asked him, 'What's the matter, lad?'

He said, 'I can't find the white mare.'

The wolf said, 'Do you see this. one, the biggest of the sheep? that is she. Go, and give her a taste of the stick.'

So the lad took and called her, and she became a horse. And he went with her to the old woman.

And the old woman said, You have two more days.'

'All right, old lady,' said the lad.

So next day also he took and went off with the mare, to try and find her. (The old woman had thrashed the mare for not hiding herself properly, so that he could not have found her. And the white mare had said, 'Forgive me, old woman. This time I will hide in the clouds, and he never will find me.')

So the lad went off with her, to try and find her; and she went into the clouds. So the lad set to work, and searched from morning till noon. And the crow came into his mind;

and, as he thought of it, the crow came and asked him, 'What's the matter, lad?'

'Why, I have lost the white mare, and cannot light on her.'

So the crow summoned all the crows, and they searched upon every side, till they lighted on her. So they took her in their beaks, and brought her to the lad. So the lad took her, and led her to the old woman.

'You have one day more,' said the old woman.

So the day came when the lad had to find the mare once more. (That night the old woman had thrashed the white mare and pretty nigh killed it. And the mare had said to the old woman, 'If he lights on me this time, old woman, you may know I have burst, for I will go right into the sea.)

So when the lad departed with her, she went into the sea. And the lad searched for her, and. it wanted but little of night. And the fish came into his mind. So the fish emerged before him and said, 'What's the matter, lad?'

'I don't know where the white mare has gone to.'

And the fish went and summoned all the fishes; and they gave up the white mare with her colt behind her. And the lad took her. He went with her to the old wife, and she said to him, 'Take, deary, whichever pleases you.'

The lad chose the youngest colt.

And the old wife said, 'Don't take that one, my lad; it isn't a good one. Take a handsomer.'

And the lad said, 'Let be.'

And the lad went further; and the colt turned a somersault, and became golden, with twenty-and-four wings. And the Serpent had none like his. And he went to his sisters, and took the three of them, and took too the Serpent-Maiden, and went with them home. Neither the Unclean Spirit nor the dragon could catch him. And he went home. So he made a marriage; and they ate and drank. And I left them there, and came and told my tale to your lordships.

No. 11.--The Two Thieves

There was a time when there was. There were two thieves. One was a country thief, and one a town thief. So the time came that the two met, and they asked one another whence they are and what they are.

Then the country thief said to the town one, 'Well, if you're such a clever thief as to be able to steal the eggs from under a crow, then I shall know that you are a thief.'

He said, 'See me, how I'll steal them.'

And he climbed lightly up the tree, and put his hand under the crow, and stole the eggs from her, and the crow never felt it. Whilst he is stealing the crow's eggs, the country thief stole his breeches, and the town thief never felt him. And when he came down and saw that he was naked, he said, 'Brother, I never felt you stealing my breeches; let's become brothers.'

So they became brothers.

Then what are they to do? They went into the city, and took one wife between them. And the town thief said, 'Brother, it is a sin for two brothers to have one wife. It were better for her to be yours.'

He said, 'Mine be she.'

'But, come now, where I shall take you, that we may get money.'

'Come on, brother, since you know.'

So they took and departed. Then they came to the king's, and considered how to get into his palace. And what did they devise?

Said the town thief, 'Come, brother, and let us break into the palace, and let ourselves down one after the other.' 'Come on.'

So they got on the palace, and broke through the roof; and the country thief lowered himself, and took two hundred purses of money, and came out. And they went home.

Then the king arose in the morning, and looked at his money, and saw that two hundred purses of money were missing. Straightway he arose and went to the prison, where was an old thief. And when he came to him, he asked him, 'Old thief, I know not who has come into my palace, and stolen from me two hundred purses of money. And I know not where they went out by, for there is no hole anywhere in the palace.'

The old thief said, 'There must be one, O king, only you don't see it. But go and make a fire in the palace, and come out and watch the palace; and where you see smoke issuing, that was where the thieves entered. And do you put a cask of molasses just there at that hole, for the thief will come again who stole the money.'

Then the king went and made a fire, and saw the hole where the smoke issues in the roof of the palace. And he went and got a cask of molasses, and put it there at the hole. Then the thieves came again there at night to that hole. And the thief from the country let himself down again; and as he did so he fell into the cask of molasses. And he said to his brother, 'Brother, it is all over with me. But, not to do the king's pleasure, come and cut off my head, for I am as good as dead.'

So his comrade lowered himself down, and cut off his head, and went and buried it in a wood.

So, when the king arose, he arose early, and went there, where the thief had fallen, and sees the thief there in the cask of molasses, and with no head. Then what is he to do? He took and went to the old thief, and told him, 'Look you, old thief, I caught the thief, and he has no head.'

Then the old thief said, 'There! O king, this is a cunning thief. But what are you to do? Why, take the corpse, and hang it up outside at the city gate. And he who stole his head will come to steal him too. And do you set soldiers to watch him.'

So the king went and took the corpse, and hung it up, and set soldiers to watch it.

Then the thief took and bought a white mare and a cart, and took a jar of twenty measures of wine. And he put it in the cart, and drove straight to the place where his comrade was hanging. He made himself very old, and pretended the cart had broken down, and the jar had

The king took the corpse, hung it up, and set soldiers to watch it

fallen out. And he began to weep and tear his hair, and he made himself to cry aloud, that he was a poor man, and his master would kill him. The soldiers guarding the corpse said one to another, 'Let's help to put this old fellow's jar in the cart, mates, for it's a pity to hear him.'

So they went to help him, and said to him, 'Hullo! old chap, we'll put your jar in the cart; will you give us a, drop to drink?'

'That I will, deary.'

So they went and put the jar in the cart. And the old fellow took and said to them, 'Take a pull, deary, for I have nothing to give it you in.'

So the soldiers took and drank till they could drink no more. And the old fellow made himself to ask, 'And who is this?'

The soldiers said, 'That is a thief.'

Then the old man said, 'Hullo! deary, I shan't spend the night here, else that thief will steal my mare.'

Then the soldiers said, 'What a silly you are, old fellow! How will he come and steal your mare?'

'He will, though, deary. Isn't he a thief?'

'Shut up, old fellow. He won't steal your mare; and if he does, we'll pay you for her.'

'He will steal her, deary; he's a thief.'

'Why, old boy, he's dead. We'll give you our written word that if he steals your mare we will pay you three hundred groats for her.'

Then the old man said, 'All right, deary, if that's the case.'

So he stayed there. He placed himself near the fire, and a drowsy fit took him, and he pretended to sleep. The soldiers kept going to the jar of wine, and drank every drop of the wine, and got drunk. And where they fell there they slept, and took no thought. The old chap, the thief, who pretended to sleep, arose and stole the corpse from the gallows, and put it on his mare, and carried it into the forest and buried it. And he left his mare there and went back to the fire, and pretended to sleep.

And when the soldiers arose, and saw that neither the corpse was there nor the old man's mare, they marvelled, and said, 'There! my comrades, the old man said rightly the thief would steal his mare. Let's make it up to him.'

So by the time the old man arose they gave him four hundred groats, and begged him to say no more about it.

Then when the king arose, and saw there was no thief on the gallows, he went to the old thief in the prison, and said to him, 'There! they have stolen the thief from the gallows, old thief. What am I to do?'

'Did not I tell you, O king, that this is a cunning thief? But do you go and buy up all the joints of meat in the city.

And charge a ducat the two pounds, so that no one will care to buy any, unless he has come into a lot of money. But that thief won't be able to hold out three days.'

Then the king went and bought up all the joints, and left one joint and that one he priced at a ducat the pound. So nobody came to buy that day. Next day the thief would stay no longer. He took a cart and put a horse in it, and drove to the meat-market. And he pretended he had damaged his cart, and lamented he had not an axe to repair it with. Then a butcher said to him, 'Here, take my axe, and mend your cart.' The axe was close to the meat. As he passed to take the axe, he picked up a big piece of meat, and stuck it under his coat. And he handed the axe back to the butcher, and departed home.

The same day comes the king, and asks the butchers, 'Have you sold any meat to any one?' They said, 'We have not sold to any one.'

So the king weighed the meat, and found it twenty pounds short. And he went to the old thief in prison, and said to him, 'He has stolen twenty pounds of meat, and no one saw him.'

'Didn't I tell you, O king, that this is a cunning thief?'

'Well, what am I to do, old thief?'

'What are you to do? Whys make a proclamation, and offer in it all the money you possess, and say he shall become king in your stead, merely to tell who he is.'

Then the king went and wrote the proclamation, just as the old thief had told him. And he posted it outside by the gate. And the thief comes and reads it, and thought how he should act. And he took his heart in his teeth and went to the king, and said, 'O king, I am the thief.'

'You are?'

'I am.'

Then the king said, 'If you it be, that I may believe you are really the man, do you see this peasant coming? Well, you must steal the ox from under the yoke without his seeing you.'

Then the thief said, 'I'll steal it, O king; watch me.' And he went before the peasant, and began to cry aloud, 'Comedy of Comedies!'

Then the peasant said, 'See there, God! Many a time have I been in the city, and have often heard "Comedy of Comedies," and have never gone to see what it is like.'

And he left his cart, and went off to the other end of the city; and the thief kept crying out till he had got the peasant some distance from the oxen. Then the thief returns, and takes the ox, and cuts off its tail, and sticks it in the mouth of the other ox, and came away with the first ox to the king. Then the king laughed fit to kill himself. The peasant, when he came back, began to weep; and the king called him and asked, 'What are you weeping for, my man?'

'Why, O king, whilst I was away to see the play, one of the oxen has gone and eaten up the other.'

When the king heard that, he laughed fit to kill himself, and he told his servant to give him two good oxen. And he gave him also his own ox, and asked him, 'Do you recognise your ox, my man?'

'I do, O king.'

'Well, away you go home.'

And he went to the thief. 'Well, my fine fellow, I will give you my daughter, and you shall become king in my stead, if you will steal the priest for me out of the church.'

Then the thief went into the town, and got three hundred crabs and three hundred candles, and went to the church, and stood up on the pavement. And as the priest chanted, the thief let out the crabs one by one, each with a candle fastened to its claw; he let it out.

And the priest said, 'So righteous am I in the sight of God that He sends His saints for me.'

The thief let out all the crabs, each with a candle fastened to its claw, and he said, 'Come, O priest, for God calls thee by His messengers to Himself, for thou art righteous.'

The priest said, 'And how am I to go?'

'Get into this sack.'

And he let down the sack; and the priest got in; and he lifted him up, and dragged him down the steps. And the priest's head went *tronk, tronk*. And he took him on his back, and carried him to the king, and tumbled him down. And the king burst out laughing. And straightway he gave his daughter to the thief, and made him king in his stead.

No. 12.--The Gypsy and the Priest

There was a very poor Gypsy, and he had many little children. And his wife went to the town, begged herself a few potatoes and a little flour. And she had no fat.

All right,' she thought; 'wait a bit. The priest has killed a pig; I'll go and beg myself a bit of fat.'

When she got there, the priest came out, took his whip, thrashed her soundly. She came home, said to her husband,' O my God, I did just get a thrashing!'

And the Gypsy is at work. Straightway the hammer fell from his hand. 'Now, wait a bit till I show him a trick, and teach him a lesson.'

The Gypsy went to the church, and took a look at the door, how to make the key to the tower. He came home, sat down at his anvil, set to work at once on the key. When he had made it, he went back to try to open the door. It opened it as though it had been made for it.

'Wait a bit, now,' he thinks to himself; 'what shall I need next?'

He went straight off to the shop, and bought himself some fine paper, just like the fine clothes the priests wear for high mass. When he had bought it, he went to the tailor, told him to make him clothes like an angel's; he looked in

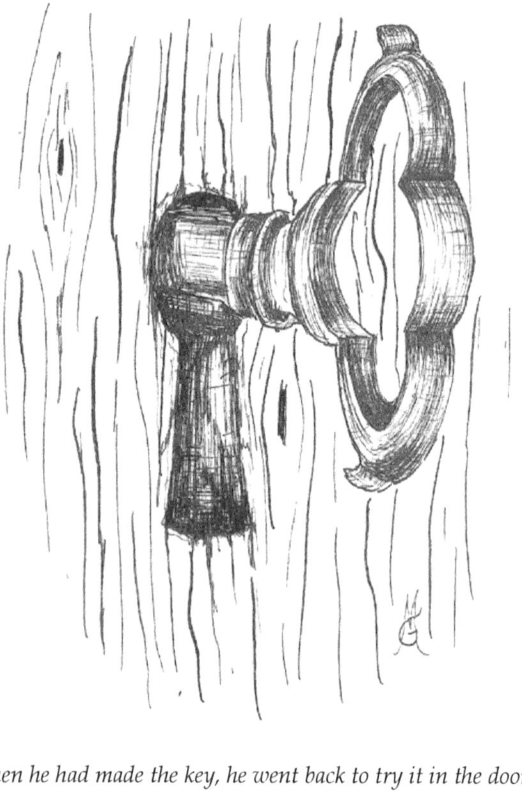

When he had made the key, he went back to try it in the door

them just like a priest. He came home, told his son (he was twenty years old), 'Hark'ee, mate, come along with me, and bring the pot. Catch about a hundred crabs. Ha! they shall see what I'll do this night; the priest won't escape with his life.'

All right!

Midnight came. The Gypsy went to the church, lit all the lights that were in the church. The cook goes to look out. 'My God! what's the matter? the whole church is lighted up.'

She goes to the priest, wakes him up. 'Get up! Let's go and see what it is. The whole church is blazing inside. What ever is it?'

The priest was in a great fright. He pulled on his vestment, and went to the church to see. The Gypsy chants like a priest performing service in the great church where the greatest folks go to service. 'Oh!' the Gypsy was chanting, 'O God, he who is a sinful man, for him am I come; him who takes so much money with him will I fetch to Paradise, and there it shall be well with him.'

When the gentleman heard that, he went home, and got all the money he had in the house.

All right!

The priest came back to the church. The Gypsy chants to him to make haste, for sooner or later the end of all things approaches. Straightway the Gypsy opened the sack, and the priest got into it. The Gypsy took all the priest's money, and hid it in his pocket.

'Good! now you are mine.'

When he closed the sack, the priest was in a great fright. 'My God! what will become of me? I know not what sort of a being that is, whether God Himself or an angel.'

The Gypsy straightway drags the priest down the steps. The priest cries that it hurts him, that he should go gently with him, for he is all broken already; that half an hour of that will kill him, for his bones are all broken already.

Well, he dragged him along the nave of the church, and pitched him down before the door; and he put a lot of thorns there to run into the priest's flesh. He dragged him backwards and forwards through the thorns, and the thorns stuck into him. When the Gypsy saw that the priest was more dead than alive, he opened the sack, and left him there.

The Gypsy went home, and threw off his disguise, and put it on the fire, that no one might say he had done the deed. The Gypsy had more than eight hundred silver pieces. So he and his wife and his children were glad that they had such a lot of money; and if the Gypsy has not died with his wife and his children, perhaps he is living still.

In the morning when the sexton comes to ring the bell, he sees a sack in front of the church. The priest was quite dead. When he opened it and saw the priest, he was in a great fright. 'What on earth took our priest in there?' He runs into the town, made a great outcry, that so and so has happened. The poor folks came and the gentry to see what was up: all the candles in the church were burning. So they buried the parson decently. If he is not rotten he is whole. May the devils still be eating him. I was there, and heard everything that happened.

NO. 13.--THE WATCHMAKER

There was once a poor lad. He took the road, went to find himself a master. He met a priest on the road. Where are you going, my lad?'

'I am going to find myself a master.'

'Mine's the very place for you, my lad, for I've another lad like you, and I have six oxen and a plough. Do you enter my service and plough all this field.'

The lad arose, and took the plough and the oxen, and went into the fields and ploughed two days. Luck and the Ogre came to him. And the Ogre said to Luck, 'Go for him.' Luck didn't want to go for him; only the Ogre went. When the Ogre went for him, he laid himself down on his back, and unlaced his boots, and took to flight across the plain.

The other lad shouted after him, 'Don't go, brother; don't go, brother.'

'Bah! God blast your plough and you as well.'

Then he came to a city of the size of Bucharest. Presently he arrived at a watchmaker's shop. And he leaned his elbows on the shop-board and watched the prentices at their work. Then one of them asked him, 'Why do you sit there hungry?'

The emperor, when he heard it,came down from his throne, and took his clock in his arms and grew young

'He said, 'Because I like to watch you working.'

Then the master came out and said, 'Here, my lad, I will hire you for three years, and will show you all that I am master of. For a year and a day,' he continued, 'you will have nothing to do but chop wood, and feed the oven fire, and sit with your elbows on the table, and watch the prentices at their work.'

Now the watchmaker had had a clock of the emperor's fifteen years, and no one could be found to repair it; he had fetched watchmakers from Paris and Vienna, and not one of them had managed it. The time came when the emperor offered the half of his kingdom to whoso should repair it; one and all they failed. The clock had twenty-four tunes in it. And as it played, the emperor grew young again. Easter Sunday came; and the watchmaker went to church with his prentices. Only the old wife and the lad stayed behind. The lad chopped the wood up quickly, and went back to the table that they did their work at. He never touched one of the little watches, but he took the big clock, and set it on the table. He took out two of its pipes, and cleaned them, and put them back in their place; then the four-and-twenty tunes began to play, and the clock to go. Then the lad hid himself for fear; and all the people came out of the church when they heard the tunes playing.

The watchmaker, too, came home, and said, 'Mother, who did me this kindness, and repaired the clock?'

His mother said, 'Only the lad, dear, went near the table.'

And he sought him and found him sitting in the stable. He took him in his arms: 'My lad, you were my master, and I never knew it, but set you to chop wood on Easter Day.' Then he sent for three tailors, and they made him three fine suits of clothes. Next day he ordered a carriage with four fine horses; and he took the clock in his arms, and went off to the emperor. The emperor, when he heard it, came down from his throne, and took his clock in his arms and grew young. Then he said to the watchmaker, 'Bring me him who mended the clock.'

He said, 'I mended it.'

'Don't tell me it was you. Go and bring me him who mended it.'

He went then and brought the lad.

The emperor said, 'Go, give the watchmaker three purses of ducats; but the lad you shall have no more, for I mean to give him ten thousand ducats a year, just to stay here and mind the clock and repair it when it goes wrong.'

So the lad dwelt there thirteen years.

The emperor had a grown-up daughter, and he proposed to find a husband for her. She wrote a letter, and gave it to her father. And what did she put in the letter? She put this: 'Father, I am minded to feign to be dumb; and whoso is able to make me speak, I will be his.'

Then the emperor made a proclamation throughout the world: 'He who is able to make my daughter speak shall get her to wife; and whoso fails him will I kill.'

Then many suitors came, but not one of them made her speak. And the emperor killed them all, and by and by no one more came.

Now the lad, the watchmaker, went to the emperor, and said, 'Emperor, let me also go to the maiden, to see if I cannot make her speak.'

'Well, this is how it stands, my lad. Haven't you seen the proclamation on the table, how I have sworn to kill whoever fails to make her speak?'

'Well, kill me also, Emperor, if I too fail.'

'In that case, go to her.'

The lad dressed himself bravely, and went into her chamber. She was sewing at her frame. When the lad entered, he said, 'Good-day, you rogue.'

Thank you, watchmaker. Well, sit you down since you have come, and take a bite.'

'Well, all right, you rogue.'

He only was speaking. Then he tarried no longer, but came out and said, 'Good-night, rogue.'

'Farewell, watchmaker.'

Next evening the emperor summoned him, to kill him. But the lad said, 'Let me go one more night.' Then the lad went again, and said, 'Good-evening, rogue.'

'Welcome, watchmaker. And since you have come, brother, pray sit down to table.'

Only he spoke, so at last he said, 'Good-night, rogue.'

'Farewell, watchmaker.'

Next night the emperor summoned him. 'I must kill you now, for you have reached your allotted term.'

Then said the lad, 'Do you know, emperor, that there is thrice forgiveness for a man?'

'Then go to-night, too.'

Then the lad went that night, and said, 'How do you do, rogue?'

'Thank you, watchmaker. Since you have come, sit at table.'

'So I will, rogue. And see you this knife in my hand? I mean to cut you in pieces if you will not answer my question.' And why should I not answer it, watchmaker?'

'Well, rogue, know you the princess?'

'And how should I not know her?'

'And the three princes, know you them?'

'I know them, watchmaker.'

'Well and good, if you know them. The three brothers had an intrigue with the princess. They knew not that the three had to do with her. But what did the maiden? She knew they were brothers. The eldest came at nightfall, and she set him down to table and he ate. Then she lay with him and shut him up in a chamber. The middle one came at midnight, and she lay with him also and shut him up in another chamber. And that same night came the youngest, and she lay with him too. Then at daybreak she let them all out, and they sprang to slay one another, the three brothers. The maiden said, "Hold, brothers, do not slay one another, but go home and take each of you to himself ten thousand ducats, and go into three cities; and his I will become who brings me the finest piece of workmanship." So the eldest journeyed to Bucharest, and there found a beautiful mirror. Now look you what kind of mirror it was. "Here, merchant, what is the price of your mirror?" "Ten thousand ducats, my lad." "Indeed, is that not very dear, brother?" "But mark you what kind of mirror it is. You look in it and you can see both the dead and the living therein." Now let's have a look at the middle brother. He went to another city and found a robe. "You, merchant, what is the price of this robe?" "Ten thousand ducats, my son."'

'What *are* you talking about, watchmaker? A robe cost ten thousand ducats!'

'But look you, you rogue, what sort of robe it is. For when you step on it, it will carry you whither you will. So you may fancy he cries "Done!" Meanwhile the youngest also arrived in a city and found a Jew, and bought an apple from him. And the apple was such that when a dead man ate it he revived. He took it and came to his brothers. And when they were all come home they saw their sweet-heart dead. And they gave her the apple to eat and she arose. And whom then did she choose? She chose the youngest. What do you say?'

And the emperor's daughter spoke. And the watchmaker took her to wife. And they made a marriage.

No. 14.--The Red King and the Witch

It was the Red King, and he bought ten ducats' worth of victuals. He cooked them, and he put them in a press. And he locked the press, and from night to night posted people to guard the victuals.

In the morning, when he looked, he found the platters bare; he did not find anything in them. Then the king said, 'I will give the half of my kingdom to whoever shall be found to guard the press, that the victuals may not go amissing from it.'

The king had three sons. Then the eldest thought within himself, 'God! What, give half the kingdom to a stranger! It were better for me to watch. Be it unto me according to God's will.'

He went to his father. 'Father, all hail. What, give the kingdom to a stranger! It were better for me to watch.'

And his father said to him, 'As God will, only don't be frightened by what you may see.'

Then he said, 'Be it unto me according to God's will.'

And he went and lay down in the palace. And he put his head on the pillow, and remained with his head on the pillow till towards dawn. And a warm sleepy breeze came and lulled him to slumber. And his little sister arose. And

The king bought ten ducats' worth of victuals and locked them away

she turned a somersault, and her nails became like an axe and her teeth like a shovel. And she opened the cupboard and ate up everything. Then she became a child again and returned to her place in the cradle, for she was a babe at the breast. The lad arose and told his father that he had seen nothing. His father looked in the press, found the platters bare--no victuals, no anything. His father said, 'It would take a better man than you, and even he might do nothing.'

His middle son also said, 'Father, all hail. I am going to watch to-night.'

'Go, dear, only play the man.'

'Be it unto me according to God's will.'

And he went into the palace and put his head on a pillow. And at ten o'clock came a warm breeze and sleep seized him. Up rose his sister and unwound herself from her swaddling-bands and turned a somersault, and her teeth became like a shovel and her nails like an axe. And she went to the press and opened it, and ate off the platters what she found. She ate it all, and turned a somersault again and went back to her place in the cradle. Day broke and the lad arose, and his father asked him and said, 'It would take a better man than you, and even he might do nought for me if he were as poor a creature as you.'

The youngest son arose. 'Father, all hail. Give me also leave to watch the cupboard by night.'

'Go, dear, only don't be frightened with what you see.'

'Be it unto me according to God's will,' said the lad.

And he went and took four needles and lay down with his head on the pillow; and he stuck the four needles in four places. When sleep seized him he knocked his head against a needle, so he stayed awake until ten o'clock. And his sister arose from her cradle, and he saw. And she turned a somersault, and he was watching her. And her teeth became like a shovel and her nails like an axe. And she went to the press and ate up everything. She left the platters bare. And she turned a somersault, and became tiny again as she was; went to her cradle. The lad, when he saw that, trembled with fear; it seemed to him ten years till daybreak. And he arose and went to his father. 'Father, all hail.'

Then his father asked him, 'Didst see anything, Peterkin?'

'What did I see? what did I not see? Give me money and a horse, a horse fit to carry the money, for I am away to marry me.'

His father gave him a couple of sacks of ducats, and he put them on his horse. The lad went and made a hole on the border of the city. He made a chest of stone, and put all the money there and buried it. He placed a stone cross above and departed. And he journeyed eight years and came to the queen of all the birds that fly.

And the queen of the birds asked him, 'Whither away, Peterkin?'

'Thither, where there is neither death nor old age, to marry me.'

The queen said to him, 'Here is neither death nor old age.'

Then Peterkin said to her, 'How comes it that here is neither death nor old age?'

Then she said to him, 'When I whittle away the wood of all this forest, then death will come and take me and old age.'

Then Peterkin said, One day and one morning death will come and old age, and take me.'

And he departed further, and journeyed on eight years and arrived at a palace of copper. And a maiden came forth from that palace and took him and kissed him. She said, 'I have waited long for thee.'

She took the horse and put him in the stable, and the lad spent the night there. He arose in the morning and placed his saddle on the horse.

Then the maiden began to weep, and asked him, 'Whither away, Peterkin?'

'Thither, where there is neither death nor old age.'

Then the maiden said to him, 'Here is neither death nor old age.'

Then he asked her, 'How comes it that here is neither death nor old age?'

Why, when these mountains are levelled, and these forests, then death will come.'

This is no place for me,' said the lad to her. And he departed further.

Then what said his horse to him? 'Master, whip me four times, and twice yourself, for you are come to the Plain of Regret. And Regret will seize you and cast you down, horse and all. So spur your horse, escape, and tarry not.'

He came to a hut. In that hut he beholds a lad, as it were ten years old, who asked him, What seekest thou, Peterkin, here?'

I seek the place where there is neither death nor old age.'

The lad said, 'Here is neither death nor old age. I am the Wind.'

Then Peterkin said, 'Never, never will I go from here.' And he dwelt there a hundred years and grew no older.

There the lad dwelt, and he went out to hunt in the Mountains of Gold and Silver, and he could scarce carry home the game.

Then what said the Wind to him? 'Peterkin, go unto all the Mountains of Gold and unto the Mountains of Silver; but go not to the Mountain of Regret or to the Valley of Grief.'

He heeded not, but went to the Mountain of Regret and the Valley of Grief. And Grief cast him down; he wept till his eyes were full.

And he went to the Wind. 'I am going home to my father, I will not stay longer.'

'Go not, for your father is dead, and brothers you have no more left at home. A million years. have come and gone since then. The spot is not known where your father's palace stood. They have planted melons on it; it is but an hour since I passed that way.'

But the lad departed thence, and arrived at the maiden's whose was the palace of copper. Only one stick remained, and she cut it and grew old. As he knocked at the door, the stick fell and she died. He buried her, and departed thence. And he came to the queen of the birds in the great forest. Only one branch remained, and that was all but through.

When she saw him she said, 'Peterkin, thou art quite young.'

Then he said to her, 'Dost thou remember telling me to tarry here?'

As she pressed and broke through the branch, she, too, fell and died.

He came where his father's palace stood and looked about him. There was no palace, no anything. And he fell to marvelling: 'God, Thou art mighty!' He only recognised his father's well, and went to it. His sister, the witch, when she saw him, said to him, 'I have waited long for you, dog.' She rushed at him to devour him, but he made the sign of the cross and she perished.

And he departed thence, and came on an old man with his beard down to his belt. 'Father, where is the palace of the Red King? I am his son.'

'What is this,' said the old man, 'thou tellest me, that thou art his son? My father's father has told me of the Red King. His very city is no more. Dost thou not see it is vanished? And dost thou tell me that thou art the Red King's son?'

'It is not twenty years, old man, since I departed from my father, and dost thou tell me that thou knowest not my father?' (It was a million years since he had left his home.) 'Follow me if thou dost not believe me.'

And he went to the cross of stone; only a palm's breadth was out of the ground. And it took him two days to get at the chest of money. When he had lifted the chest out and opened it, Death sat in one corner groaning, and Old Age groaning in another corner.

Then what said Old Age? 'Lay hold of him, Death.'

'Lay hold of him yourself.'

Old Age laid hold of him in front, and Death laid hold of him behind.

The old man took and buried him decently, and planted the cross near him. And the old man took the money and also the horse.

No. 15.--The Prince and the Wizard

There was a king, and he had an only son. Now, that lad was heroic, nought-heeding. And he set out in quest of heroic achievements. And he went a long time nought-heeding. And he came to a forest, and lay down to sleep in the shadow of a tree, and slept. Then he saw a dream, that he arises and goes to the hill where the dragon's horses are, and that if you keep straight on you will come to the man with no kidneys, screaming and roaring. So he arose and departed, and came to the man with no kidneys. And when he came there, he asked him, 'Mercy! what are you screaming for?'

He said, 'Why, a wizard has taken my kidneys, and has left me here in the road as you see me.'

Then the lad said to him, 'Wait a bit longer till I return from somewhere.'

And he left him, and journeyed three more days and three nights. And he came to that hill, and sat down, and ate, and rested. And he arose and went to the hill. And the horses, when they saw him, ran to eat him. And the lad said, 'Do not eat me, for I will give you pearly hay and fresh water.'

Then the horses said, 'Be our master. But see you do as you've promised.'

The lad took his heroic club and hurled it

The lad said, 'Horses, if I don't, why, eat me and slay me.'

So he took them and departed with them home. And he put them in the stable, and gave them fresh water and pearly hay. And he mounted the smallest horse, and set out for the man with no kidneys, and found him there. And he asked him what was the name of the wizard who had taken his kidneys.

'What his name is I know not, but I do know where he is gone to. He is gone to the other world.'

Then the lad took and went a long time nought-heeding, and came to the edge of the earth, and let himself down, and came to the other world. And he went to the wizard's there, and said, 'Come forth, O wizard, that I may see the sort of man you are.'

So when the wizard heard, he came forth to eat him and slay him. Then the lad took his heroic club and his sabre; and the instant he hurled his club, the wizard's hands were bound behind his back. And the lad said to him, 'Here, you wizard, tell quick, my brother's kidneys, or I slay thee this very hour.'

And the wizard said, 'They are there in a jar. Go and get them.'

And the lad said, 'And when I've got them, what am I to do with them?'

The wizard said, 'Why, when you've got them, put them in water and give him them to drink.'

Then the lad went and took them, and departed to him.

And he put the kidneys in water, and gave him to drink, and he drank. And when he had drunk he was whole. And he took the lad, and kissed him, and said, 'Be my brother till my death or thine, and so too in the world to come.'

So they became brothers. And having done so, they took and journeyed in quest of heroic achievements. So they set out and slew every man that they found in their road. Then the man who had had no kidneys said he was going after the wizard, and would pass to the other world. Then they took and went there to the edge of the earth, and let themselves in. And they came there, and went to the wizard. And when they got there, how they set themselves to fight, and fought with him two whole days. Then when the lad, his brother, took and hurled his club, the wizard's hands were bound behind his back. And he cut his throat, and took his houses, made them two apples.

And they went further, and came on a certain house, and there were three maidens. And the lad hurled his club, and carried away half their house. And when the maidens saw that, they came out, and saw them coming. And they flung a comb on their path, and it became a forest--no needle could thread it. So when the lad saw that, he flung his club and his sabre. And the sabre cut and the club battered. And it cut all the forest till nothing was left.

And when the maidens saw that they had felled the forest, they flung a whetstone, and it became a fortress of stone, so that there was no getting further. And he flung the club, and demolished the stone, and made dust of it. And when the maidens saw that they had demolished the stone, they flung a mirror before them, and it became a lake, and there was no getting over. And the lad flung his sabre, and it cleft the water, and they passed through, and went there to the maidens. When they came there they said, 'And what were you playing your cantrips on us for, maidens?'

Then the maidens said, 'Why, lad, we thought that you were coming to kill us.'

Then the lad shook hands with them, the three sisters, and said to them, 'There, maidens, and will you have us?'

And they took them to wife--one for himself, and one for him who had lost his kidneys, and one they gave to another lad. And he went with them home. And they made a marriage.

And I came away, and I have told the story.

NO. 16.--THE APPLES OF PREGNANCY

There were where there were a king and a queen. Now for sixteen years that king and that queen had had no sons or daughters. So he thought they would never have any. And he was always weeping and lamenting, for what would become of them without any children? Then the king said to the queen, 'O queen, I will go away and leave you, and if I do not find a son born of you by my return, know that either I will kill you with my own hands, or I will send you away, and live no longer with you.'

Then another king sent a challenge to him to go and fight, for, if he goes not, he will come and slay him on his throne. Then the king said to his queen, 'Here, O queen, is a challenge come for me to go and fight. If I had had a son, would he not have gone, and I have remained at home?'

She said, 'How can I help it, O king, if God has not chosen to give us any sons? What can I do?'

He said, 'Prate not to me of God. If I come and don't find a son born of you, I shall kill you.'

And the king departed.

Then the holy God and St. Peter fell to discussing what they should do for the queen. So God said to Peter, 'Here, you Peter, go down with this apple, and pass before her window, and cry, "I have an apple, and whoso eats of it

The Apples of Pregnancy

will conceive." She will hear you. For it were a pity, Peter, for the king to come and kill her.'

So St. Peter took the apple, and came down, and did as God had told him. He cried in front of the queen's window. She heard him, and came out, and called him to her, and asked, 'How much do you want for that apple, my man?'

He said, 'I want much; give me a purse of money.'

And the queen took the purse of money, and gave it him, and took the apple and ate it. And when she had eaten it, she conceived. And St. Peter left her the purse of money there. So the time drew near for her to bear a child. And the very day that she brought forth her son, his father came from the war, and he had won the fight. So when he came home and heard that the queen had borne him a son, he went to the wine-shop and drank till he was drunk. And as he was coming home from the wine-shop, he reached the door, and fell down, and died. Then the boy heard it, and rose up out of his mother's arms, and went to the vintner, and killed him with a blow. And he came home. And the people, the nobles, beheld him, what a hero he was, and wondered at him. But an evil eye fell on him, and for three days he took to his bed. And he died of the evil eye.

CHAPTER III

BUKOWINA GYPSY STORIES

NO. 17.--IT ALL COMES TO LIGHT

THERE was a man with as many children as ants in an anthill. And three of the girls went to reap corn, and the emperor's son came by. And the eldest girl said, 'If the emperor's son will marry me, I will clothe his whole army with one spindleful of thread.' And the middle girl said, 'I will feed his army with a single loaf.' And the youngest girl said, 'If he will marry me, I will bear him twins clever and good, with hair of gold and teeth like pearls.'

His servant heard them. 'Emperor, the eldest girl said, if you will marry her, she will clothe your army with one spindleful of thread; the middle girl said, if you will marry her, she will feed your army with a single loaf; the youngest girl said, if you will marry her, she will bear you twins clever and good, with golden hair.'

'Turn back,' he cried, 'take the youngest girl, put her in the carriage.'

He brought her home; he lived with her half a year; and they summoned him to the army to fight. He remained a year at the war. His empress brought forth two sons. The servant took them, and flung them into the pigstye; and she put two whelps by the mother.

At evening the pigs came home, and the eldest sow cried, 'Hah! here are our master's sons; quick, give them the teat to suck, and keep them warm.'

The pigs went forth to the field. The servant came, saw that the boys are well, not dead; she flung them into the stable. At evening the horses came home, and the eldest mare cried, 'Hah! here are our master's sons; quick, give them the teat to suck.'

In the morning the horses went forth to the field. The servant took them, and buried them in the dunghill. And two golden fir-trees grew.

The emperor came from the war. The servant went to meet him. 'Emperor, the empress has borne you a couple of whelps.'

The emperor buried the empress behind the door up to the waist, and set the two whelps to suck her. He married the servant. This servant said to the emperor, 'Fell these fir-trees, and make me a bed.'

'Fell them I will not; they are of exquisite beauty.'

'If you don't, I shall die.'

The emperor set men to work, and felled the firs, and gathered all the chips, and burned them with fire. He made a bed of the two planks, and slept with his new empress in the bed.

And the elder boy said, 'Brother, do you feel it heavy, brother?'

'No, I don't feel it heavy, for my father is sleeping on me; but you, do you feel it heavy, brother?'

'I do, for my stepmother is sleeping on me.'

She heard, she arose in the morning. 'Emperor, chop up this bed, and put it in the fire, that it be burnt.'

'Burn it I will not.'

'But you must put it in the fire, else I shall die.'

The emperor bade them put it in the fire. She bade them block up the chimney, that not a spark should escape. But two sparks escaped, and fell on a couple of lambs: the lambs became golden. She saw, and commanded the servants to kill the lambs. She gave the servants the chitterlings to wash them, and gave the chitterlings numbered. They were washing them in the stream; two of the chitterlings fell into the water. They cut two chitterlings in half, and added them to the number, and came home. From those two chitterlings which fell into the water came two doves; and they turned a somersault, and became boys. And they went to a certain lady. This lady was a widow, and she took the boys in, and brought them up seven years, and clothed them.

And the emperor made proclamation in the land that they should gather to him to a ball. All Bukowina assembled. They ate and drank. The emperor said, 'Guess what I have suffered.' Nobody guessed. These two boys also went, and sat at the gate. The emperor saw them. 'Call also these two boys.'

They called them to the emperor. 'What are you come for, boys?'

'We came, emperor, to guess.'

'Well, guess away.'

There was a man with children as many as ants in an anthill. And three of the girls went to reap corn, and the emperor's son came by. And the eldest girl said, "If this lad will marry me, I will clothe his army with one spindleful of thread." The middle girl said, "If he will marry me, I will feed his army with a single loaf." The youngest girl said, "If this emperor's son will marry me, I will bear him twins clever and good, with hair of gold and teeth like pearls." His servant said to the emperor, "Emperor, the eldest girl said that, if you will marry her, she will clothe your army with one spindleful of thread; and the middle girl said, if you will marry her, she will feed your army with a single loaf; and the youngest girl said, if you will marry her, she will bear you twins clever and good, with hair of gold and teeth like pearls." Come forth, pearl. The emperor lived with her half a year, and departed to war, and remained a year. The empress brought forth two sons. The servant took them, flung them into the pigstye, and put two whelps by her. At evening the pigs came home, and the eldest sow cried, "Hah! here are our master's sons; you must give them the teat." In the morning the pigs went forth to the field. The servant came, saw that they are well, flung them into the stable. At evening the horses came; the eldest horse cried, "Hah! here are our master's sons; you must give them the teat." In the morning the horses went forth to the field. She came and saw that they are well. She buried them in the horses' dunghill, and two golden fir-trees grew. The emperor came from the army. The servant went to meet him. "Emperor, the empress has borne a couple of whelps." The emperor buried her behind the door, and set the two whelps to suck. The emperor married the servant. The new empress said, "Fell the fir-trees, and make a bed." "Fell them I will not, for they are beautiful." "If you don't fell them, I shall die." The emperor commanded, and they felled them, and he gathered all the chips and flung them in the fire, and he made a bed. And the emperor was sleeping in the bed with the servant. And the elder brother said, "Do you feel it heavy, brother?" "No, I don't feel it heavy, for my true father is sleeping on me; but do you feel it heavy, brother?" "I do, for my stepmother is sleeping on me." She heard, she arose in the morning. "Emperor, chop up this bed, and put it in the fire." "Chop it up I will not, for it is fair." "If you don't, I shall die." The emperor commanded, and chopped up the bed, and they put it in the fire; and she told them to block up the chimney. But two sparks jumped out on two lambs, and the lambs became golden. She saw, and commanded the servants to kill them, and gave the chitterlings to two girls to wash. And two chitterlings escaped, and they cut two chitterlings, and made up the proper number. From those chitterlings came two doves; and they turned a somersault, and became two boys. And they went to a

The two doves became two boys

certain widow lady, and she took them in, and brought them up seven years. The emperor gathered Bukowina to a ball, and they ate and drank. The emperor told them to guess what he had suffered. Nobody guessed, but I have. And if you believe not, we are your sons, and our mother is buried behind the door.'

Then came his mother into the hall. 'Good-day to you, my sons.'

'Thank you, mother.'

And they took that servant, and bound her to a wild horse, and gave him his head, and he smashed her to pieces.

No. 18.--The Golden Children

There were three princesses, and they vaunted themselves before the three princes. One vaunted that she will make him a golden boy and girl. And one vaunted that she will feed his army with one crust of bread. And one vaunted that she will clothe the whole army with a single spindleful of thread. The time came that the princes took the three maidens. So she who had vaunted that she will bear the golden boy and girl, the time came that she grew big with child, and she fell on the hearth in the birth-pangs. The midwife came and his mother, and she brought forth a golden boy and girl. And her man was not there. And the midwife and his mother took a dog and a bitch, and put them beneath her. And they took the boy and the girl, and the midwife threw them into the river. And they went floating on the river, and a monk found them.

So their father went a-hunting, and their father found the lad. 'Let me kiss you.' For, he thought, My wife said she would bear a golden lad and girl like this. And he came home and fell sick; and the midwife noticed it and his mother.

The midwife asked him, 'What ails you?'

He said, 'I am sick, because I have seen a lad like my wife said she would bear me.'

Then she sent for the children, did his mother; and the monk brought them; and she asked him, 'Where did you get those children?'

He said, 'I found them both floating on the river.'

And the king saw it must be his children; his heart yearned towards them. So the king called the monk, and asked him, 'Where did you get those children?'

He said, 'I found them floating on the river.'

He brought the monk to his mother and the midwife, and said, 'Behold, mother, my children.'

She repented and said, 'So it is.' She said, 'Yes, darling, the midwife put them in a box, and threw them into the water.'

Then he kindled the furnace, and cast both his mother and also the midwife into the furnace. And he burnt them; and so they made atonement. He gathered all the kings together, for joy that he had found his children. Away I came, the tale have told.

No. 19.--The Two Children

Somewhere there was a hunter's son, a soldier; and there was also a shoemaker's daughter. She had a dream that if he took her to wife, and if she fell pregnant by him, she would bring forth twins--the boy with a golden star upon his breast, and the girl with a golden star upon the brow. And he presently took her to wife. And she was poor, that shoemaker's daughter; and he was rich. So his parents did not like her for a daughter-in-law. She became with child to him; and he went off to serve as a soldier. Within a year she brought forth. When that befell, she had twins exactly as she had said. She bore a boy and a girl; the boy had a golden star upon his breast, and the girl had a golden star upon her brow. But his parents threw the twins into diamond chests, wrote a label for each of them, and put it in the chest. Then they let them swim away down the Vah river.

Then my God so ordered it, that there were two fishers, catching fish. They saw those chests come swimming down the river; they laid hold of both of them. When they had done so, they opened the chests, and there were the children alive, and on each was the label with writing. The fishers took them up, and went straight to the church to baptize them.

So those children lived to their eighth year, and went already to school. And the fishers had also children of their own, and used to beat them, those foundlings. He, the boy, was called Jankos; and she, Marishka:

God so ordered it that two fishermen saw the chests and laid hold of both

And Marishka said to Jankos, 'Let us go, Jankos mine, somewhere into the world.'

Then they went into a forest, there spent the night. There they made a fire, and Marishka fell into a slumber, whilst he, Jankos, kept up the fire. There came a very old stranger to him, and he says to him, says that stranger, 'Come with me, Jankos, I will give you plenty of money.'

He brought him into a vault; there a stone door opened before him; the vault was full, brim full of money. Jankos took two armfuls of money. It was my God who was there with him, and showed him the money. He took as much as he could carry, then returned to Marishka. Marishka was up already and awake; she was weeping--'Where, then, is Jankos?'

Jankos calls to her, 'Fear not, I am here; I am bringing you plenty of money.'

My God had told him to take as much money as he wants; the door will always be open to him. Then they, Jankos and Marishka, went to a city; he bought clothes for himself and for her, and bought himself a fine house. Then he bought also horses and a small carriage. Then he went to the vault for that money, and helped himself again. With the shovel he flung it on the carriage; then he returned home with so much money that he didn't know what to do with it.

Then he ordered a band to play music, and arranged for a ball. Then he invited all the gentry in that country, invited all of them; and his parents too came. This he did that he might find out who were his parents. Right enough they came; and he, Jankos, at once knew his mother—my God had ordained it, that he at once should know her. Then he asks his mother, does Jankos, what a man deserved who ruins two souls, and is himself alive.

And she says, the old lady, 'Such a one deserves nothing better than to have light set to the fagot-pile, and himself pitched into the fire.'

That was just what they did to them, pitched them into the fire; and he remained there with Marishka. And the gentleman cried then, 'Hurrah! bravo! that's capital.'

No. 20.--Mare's Son

A priest went riding on his mare to town. And . . . . he led her into the forest, and left her there. The mare brought forth a son. And God came and baptized him, and gave him the name 'Mare's Son.' He sucked one year, and went to a tree, and tries to pluck it up, and could not.

'Ah! mother, I'll suck one year more.'

He sucked one year more; he went to the tree; he plucked it up.

'Now, mother, I shall go away from you.'

And he went into the forests, and found a man. 'Good day to you.'

'Thanks.'

'What's your name?'

'Tree-splitter.'

'Hah! let's become brothers. Come with me.'

They went further; they found another man. 'Good day'

'Thanks.'

'What's your name?'

'Rock-splitter.'

'Hah! let's become brothers.'

They became brothers.

'Come with me.'

They went further; they found yet another man. 'Good day to you.'

'Thanks.'

What's your name?'

'Tree-bender.'

'Come with me.'

The four went further, and they found a robbers' den. The robbers had killed a heifer. When the robbers saw them, they fled. They went away, and left the meat untouched. They cooked the meat and ate. They passed the night. In the morning Mare's Son said, 'Let three of us go to hunt, and one stay at home to cook.' They left Tree-splitter at home to cook, and he cooked the food nicely. And there came an old man to him, a hand's-breadth tall, with a beard a cubit in length.

'Give me to eat.'

'Not I. For they'll come from hunting, and there'll be nothing to give them.'

The old man went into the wood, and cut four wedges, and threw him, Tree-splitter, on the ground, and fastened him to the earth by the hands and feet, and ate up all the food. Then he let him go, and departed. He put more meat in the pot to cook. They came from hunting and asked, 'Have you cooked the food?'

'Ever since you've been away I've had the meat at the fire, but it isn't cooked properly.'

'Dish it up as it is, for we're hungry.'

He dished it up as it was, and they ate it. They passed the night. The next day they left another cook, and the three of them went off to hunt. The old man came again.

'Give me something to eat.'

'Not I, for they'll come from hunting, and there'll be nothing to give them to eat.'

He went into the wood, and cut four wedges, and fastened him to the earth by the hands and feet, and ate up all the food, and let him go, and departed. He put more meat in the pot to cook. They came from hunting. 'Have you cooked the food?'

'Ever since you've been away I've had it at the fire, but it isn't cooked, for it's old meat.'

They passed the night. The third day they left another cook. The three of them went to hunt; and those two never told what they had undergone. Again the old man came, demanded food.

'Not a morsel, for they'll come from hunting, and I should have nothing to give them.'

He went into the wood, and cut four wedges, and fastened him to the earth by the hands and feet, and ate up all the food, and let him go. They came from hunting. 'Have you cooked the food?'

'The minute you went away I put the meat in the pot but it isn't cooked, for it's old.'

The fourth day Mare's Son remained as cook, and he cooked the food nicely.

The old man came. 'Give me something to eat, for I'm hungry.'

'Come here, and I'll give you some.'

He called him into the house, and caught him by the beard, and led him to a beech-tree, and drove his axe into the beech, and cleft it, and put his beard in the cleft, and drew out the axe, and drove in wedges by the beard, and left him there. They came from hunting; he gave them to eat. ' Why didn't you cook as good food as I?'

They ate.

The old man pulled the tree out of the earth on to his shoulders, and dragged it after him, and departed into a cave in the other world.

Said Mare's Son to them, 'Come with me, and you shall see what I've caught.'

They went, and found only the place.

Said Mare's Son, 'Come with me, for I've got to find him.'

They went, following the track of the tree to his cave.

'This is where he went in. Who'll go in to fetch him out?'

They said, 'Not we, we're afraid. Do you go in, for it was you who caught him.'

He said, 'I'll go in, and do you swear that you will act fairly by me.'

They swore that they will act fairly by him. They made a basket, and he lowered himself into the cave, and went to the other world. There was a palace under the earth, and he found the old man with his beard in the tree, put him in the basket, and they drew him up. He found a big stone, and put it in the basket. 'If they pull up the stone, they will pull up me.' They pulled it up half-way, and cut the rope He fell a-weeping. 'Now I am undone.'

He journeyed under the earth, and came to a house. There was an old man and an old woman, both blind, for the

They lowered him into a cave

fairies had put out their eyes. Mare's Son went to them and said, 'Good day.'

'Thanks. And who are you?'

'I am a man.'

'And old or young?'

'Young.'

'Be a son to us.'

'Good.'

The old man had ten sheep. 'Here take the sheep, and graze them, daddy's darling. And don't go to the right hand, else the fairies will catch you and put out your eyes; that's their field. But go to the left hand, for they've no business there; that's our field.'

He went three days to the left hand, until he bethought himself, and made a flute, and went to the right hand with his sheep.

And there met him a fairy, and said to him, 'Son of a roarer, what are you wanting here?'

He began to play on the flute. 'Dance a bit for me.'

He began to play, and she danced. Just as she was dancing her very best, he broke the flute with his teeth.

The fairy said, 'What are you doing, why did you break it, when I was dancing my very best?'

'Come with me to that tree, that maple, that I may take out its heart and make a flute. And I will play all day, and you shall dance. Come with me.'

He went to the maple, and drove his axe into the maple, and cleft it. 'Put your hand in, and take out the heart.'

She put in her hand; he drew out the axe, and left her hand in the tree.

She cried, 'Quick, release my hand; it will be crushed.'

And he said, 'Where are the old man's and the old woman's eyes? For if you don't tell me, I shall cut your throat.'

'Go to the third room. They're in a glass. The larger are the old man's, the smaller the old woman's.'

'How shall I put them in again?'

'There is water in a glass there, and moisten them with the water, and put them in, and they will adhere. And smear with the water, and they will see.'

He cut her throat, and went and got the eyes of the old man and the old woman, and took the water, and moistened them with the water, and put them in, and they adhered. He smeared with the water, and they saw.

The old man and the old woman said, 'Thank you, my son. Be my son for ever. I will give all things into your hand, and I will go to my kinsfolk, for it is ten years since I have seen them.'

And the old man mounted a goat, and the old woman mounted a sheep; and he said to his son, 'Daddy's darling, walk, eat, and drink.' Away went the old man and the old woman to their kinsfolk.

He too set out, and went walking in the forest. In a tree were young eagles, and a dragon was climbing up to devour them. And Mare's Son saw him, and climbed up, and killed him.

And the young eagles said to him, 'God will give you good luck for killing him. For my mother said every year she was hatching chicks, and this dragon was always devouring them. But where shall we hide you? for our mother will come and devour you. But put yourself under us, and we will cover you with our wings.'

Their mother came. 'I smell fresh man.'

'No, mother, you just fancy it. You fly aloft, and the reek mounts up to you.'

'I'm certain there's a man here. And who killed the dragon?'

'I don't know, mother.'

'Show him, that I may see him.'

'He's among us, mother.'

They produced him, and she saw him; and the minute she saw him, she swallowed him. The eaglets began to weep and to lament: 'He saved us from death, and you have devoured him.'

'Wait a bit; I'll bring him up again.'

She brought him up, and asked him, 'What do you want for saving my young ones from death?'

'I only want you to carry me to the other world.'

'Had I known that, I'd have let him devour my young ones, for to carry you up is mighty difficult. Do you know how I shall manage it? Bake twelve ovenfuls of bread, and take twelve heifers and twelve jars of wine.'

In three days he had them ready.

She said, 'Put them on me; and when I turn my head to the left, throw a heifer into my mouth and an ovenful of bread; and when I turn to the right, pour a jar of wine into my mouth.'

She brought him out; he went to his brothers. 'Good day to you, brothers. You fancied I should perish. If you acted fairly by me, toss your arrows up in the air, and they will fall before you; but if unfairly, then they will fall on your heads.'

All four tossed up their arrows, and they stood in a row. His fell right before him, and theirs fell on their heads, and they died.

No. 21.--The Deluded Dragon

There was an old man with a multitude of children. He had an underground cave in the forest. He said, 'Make me a honey-cake, for I will go and earn something.' He went into the forest, and found a well. By the well was a table. He laid the cake on the table. The crows came and ate it. He slept by the well. He arose and saw the flies eating the crumbs. He struck a blow and killed a hundred flies. He wrote that he had killed a hundred souls with one blow. And he lay down and slept.

A dragon came with a buffalo's skin to draw water. He saw what was written on the table, that he had killed a hundred souls. When he saw the old man, he feared. The old man awoke, and he too feared.

The dragon said, 'Let's become brothers.'

And they swore that they would be Brothers of the Cross. The dragon drew water. 'Come with me, brother, to my palace.'

They went along a footpath, the old man first. When the dragon panted, he drove the old man forward; when he drew in his breath, he pulled him back. The dragon said, 'Brother, why do you sometimes run forward and sometimes come back?'

'I am thinking whether to kill you.'

The dragon climbed into the cherry tree

'Stay, brother, I will go first and you behind; maybe you will change your mind.'

They came to a cherry-tree. 'Here, brother, have some cherries.'

The dragon climbed up, and the old man was eating below. The dragon said, 'Come up, they're better here.'

The old man said, 'No, they aren't, for the birds have defiled them.'

'Catch hold of this bough.'

The old man did so. The dragon let go of it, and jerked the old man up, and he fell on a hare and caught it.

The dragon said, 'What's the matter, brother? Was the bough too strong for you?'

'I sprang of my own accord, and caught this hare. I hadn't time to run round, so up I sprang.'

The dragon came down and went home. The old man said, 'Would you like a present, sister-in-law?' [seemingly offering the hare to the dragon's wife].

'Thanks, brother-in-law.'

The dragon said to her aside, 'Don't say a word to him, else he'll kill us, for he has killed a hundred souls with one blow.' He sent him to fetch water: 'Go for water, brother.'

He took the spade and the buffalo's hide, dragged it after him, and went to the well, and was digging all round the well.

The dragon went to him. 'What are you doing, brother?'

'I am digging the whole well to carry it home.'

'Don't destroy the spring; I'll draw the water myself.'

The dragon drew the water, and took the old man by the hand, and led him home. He sent him to the forest to fetch a tree. He stripped off bark, and made himself a rope, and bound the trees.

The dragon came. 'What are you doing, brother?'

'I am going to take the whole forest and carry it home.'

'Don't destroy my forest, brother. I'll carry it myself.' The dragon took a tree on his shoulders, and went home.

He said to his wife, 'What shall we do, wife, for he will kill us if we anger him?'

She said, 'Take uncle's big club, and hit him on the head.'

The old man heard. He slept of a night on a bench. And he took the beetle, put it on the bench, dressed it up in his coat, and put his cap on the top of it. And he lay down under the bench. The dragon took the club, and felt the cap, and struck with the club. The old man arose, removed the beetle, put it under the bench, and lay down on the bench. He scratched his head. 'God will punish you, brother, and your household, for a flea has bitten me on the head.'

'There! do you hear, wife? I hit him on the head with the club, and he says a mere flea has bitten him. What shall we do with him, wife?'

Give him a sackful of money to go away.'

'What will you take to go, brother? I'll give you a sackful of money.'

'Give it me.'

He gave it. 'Take it, brother, and be gone.'

'I brought my present myself; do you carry yours yourself.'

The dragon took it on his shoulders and carried it. They drew near to the underground cavern. The old man said, 'Stay here, brother, whilst I go home and tie up the dogs, else they'll wholly devour you.' The old man went home to his children, and made them wooden knives, and told them to say when they saw the dragon, 'Mother, father's bringing a dragon; we'll eat his flesh.'

The dragon heard them, and flung down the sack, and fled. And he met a fox.

'Where are you flying to, dragon?'

'The old man will kill me.'

'Fear not; come along with me. I'll kill him, he's so weak.'

The children came outside and cried, 'Mother, the fox is bringing us the dragon skin he owes us, to cover the cave with.'

The dragon took to flight, and caught the fox, and dashed him to the earth; and the fox died. The old man went to the town, and got a cart, and put the money in it. Then he went to the town, and built himself houses, and bought himself oxen and cows.

No. 22.--The Gypsy and the Dragon

There were a Gypsy and a shepherd, who tended his sheep. Every night two of the shepherd's sheep went a-missing, or even three. The peasant came to his gossip, the Gypsy, who asks him, 'Hallo! gossip, what's up with you, that you're so sorrowful?'

The peasant says to the Gypsy, 'Ah! how should I not be sorrowful, when some one--I know not who--does me grievous harm?'

'All right. I'll help you there, for I know fine who it is. To-night let your wife make me two big cheeses, the size of that; and let her bake me some nice fine dough for supper. I'll come and sup with you to-night. Then I'll go and look after your sheep.'

All right! The Gypsy went and had a fine blow-out at the peasant's. Night came, and the Gypsy went off to the sheep. And the cheese he put in his pocket, and in his hand he took an iron bar weighing three hundredweight, besides which he made himself quite a light wooden rod. And off he went to the sheepfold. There was nobody there but the shepherd's man.

'Go you home, my lad,' says the Gypsy, 'and I'll stop here.'

Midnight came. The Gypsy made himself a big fire, and straightway the dragon comes to the Gypsy by the fire.

He said to him, 'Wait a bit. I'll give it your mother for this; what are you wanting here?'

'Just wanting to see if you are such a strong chap, though you do eat three sheep every night.'

He was terrified.

'Sit down beside me by the fire, and let's just have a little trial of strength, to see which of us is the stronger. Do you throw this stick so high up in the air that it never falls down again, but stays there.' (It was the bar that weighed three hundredweight.)

The dragon throws, threw it so high, that then and there it remained somewhere or other up in the sky. 'Now,' says the dragon to the Gypsy, 'now do you throw, as I threw.'

The Gypsy threw--it was the little light wooden stick--threw it somewhere or other behind him, so that the dragon couldn't see where he threw it, but he fancied he had thrown it where he had thrown his own.

'Well, all right! Let's sit down, and see whether you really are a clever chap. Just take this stone and squeeze it so that the water runs out of it, and the blood, like this.' The Gypsy took the cheese; he squeezed it till the water ran out of it; then he said to the dragon, 'Do you take it now and squeeze.'

He handed him a stone, and the dragon kept squeezing and squeezing till the blood streamed from his hand. 'I see plainly,' he said to the Gypsy, 'you're a better man than I.'

'Well, take me now on your back, and carry me to your blind mother.'

They came to his blind mother. Fear seized her, for where did one ever hear the like of that--the dragon to carry the Gypsy on his back.

'Now, you'll give me just whatever I want.'

'Fear not. I will give you as much money as you can carry, and as much food as you want, both to eat and to drink; only let me live and my mother. And I'll never go after the sheep any more.'

'Well and good. I could kill you this moment, and your blind mother too. Then swear to me that you will go no more to that peasant's to devour his sheep.'

Straightway he swore to him, that indeed he would go no more.

'Now you must give me money, both gold and silver, and then you must take me on your back and carry me home.'

Well and good. He gave him the money, and took him on his back, and carried home the Gypsy and the money. The Gypsy's wife sees them. 'My God! What's up?' And the children-he had plenty--came running out. The dragon was dreadfully frightened and ran off. But he flung down the Gypsy's money and left it there. The Gypsy was so rich there was not his equal. He was just like a gentle-man. And if he is not dead, he is still living, with his wife and children.

There in the earth was a palace

No. 23.--The Seer

They say that there was an emperor, and he had three sons. And he gave a ball; all Bukowina came to it. And a mist descended, and there came a dragon, and caught up the empress, and carried her into the forests to a mountain, and set her down on the earth. There in the earth was a palace. Now after the ball the men departed home.

And the youngest son was a seer; and his elder brothers said he was mad. Said the youngest, 'Let us go after our mother, and seek for her in Bukowina.' The three set out, and they came to a place where three roads met. And the youngest said, 'Brothers, which road will you go?'

And the eldest said, 'I will keep straight on.'

And the middle one went to the right, and the youngest to the left. The eldest one went into the towns, and the middle one into the villages, and the youngest into the forests. They had gone a bit when the youngest turned back and cried, 'Come here. How are we to know who has found our mother? Let us buy three trumpets, and whoever finds her must straightway blow a blast, and we shall hear him, and return home.'

The youngest went into the forests. And he was hungry, and he found an apple-tree with apples, and he ate an apple, and two horns grew. And he said, 'What God has

The Seer

given me I will bear.' And he went onward, and crossed a stream, and the flesh fell away from him. And he kept saying,' What God has given me I will bear. Thanks be to God.' And he went further, and found another apple-tree. And he said, 'I will eat one more apple, even though two more horns should grow.' When he ate it the horns dropped off. And he went further, and again found a stream. And he said, 'God, the flesh has fallen from me, now will my bones waste away; but even though they do, yet will I go.' And he crossed the stream; his flesh grew fairer than ever. And he went up into a mountain. There was a rock of stone in a spot bare of trees. And he reached out his hand, and moved it aside, and saw a hole in the earth. He put the rock back in its place, and went back and began to wind his horn.

His brothers heard him and came. 'Have you found my mother?'

'I have; come with me.'

And they went to the mountain to the rock of stone.

'Remove this rock from its place.'

'But we cannot.'

'Come, I will remove it.'

He put his little finger on it, and moved it aside. 'Hah!' said he, 'here is our mother. Who will let himself down?' And they said, 'Not I.'

The youngest said, 'Come with me into the forest, and we will strip off bark and make a rope.'

They did so, and they made a basket.

I will lower myself down, and when I jerk the rope haul me up.'

So he let himself down, and came to house No. 1. There he found an emperor's daughter, whom the dragon had brought and kept prisoner.

And she said, 'Why are you here? The dragon will kill you when he comes.'

And he asked her, 'Didn't the dragon bring an old lady here?'

And she said, 'I know not, but go to No. 2; there is my middle sister.'

He went to her; she too said, 'Why are you here? The dragon will kill you when he comes.'

And he asked, 'Didn't he bring an old lady?'

And she said, 'I know not, but go to No. 3; there is my youngest sister.'

She said, 'Why are you here? The dragon will kill you when he comes.'

And he asked, 'Didn't he bring an old lady here?' And she said, 'He did, to No. 4.'

He went to his mother, and she said, 'Why are you here? The dragon will kill you when he comes.'

And he said, 'Fear not, come with me.' And he led her, and put her in the basket, and said to her, 'Tell my brothers they've got to pull up three maidens.' He jerked the rope, and they hauled their mother up. He put the eldest girl in the basket, and they hauled her up; then the middle one, jerked the rope, and they hauled her up. And while they are hauling, he made the youngest swear that she will not marry 'till I come.' She swore that she will not marry till he comes; he put her also in the basket, jerked the rope, and they hauled her up.

And he found a stone, and put it in the basket, and jerked the rope. 'If they haul up the stone, they will also haul up me.' And they hauled it half-way up, and the rope broke, and they left him to perish, for they thought he was in the basket. And he began to weep. And he went into the palace where the dragon dwelt, and pulled out a box, and found a rusty ring. And he is cleaning it; out of it came a lord, and said, 'What do you want, master?'

'Carry me out into the world.'

And he took him up on his shoulders, and carried him out. And he took two pails of water. When he washed himself with one, his face was changed; and when with the other, it became as it was before. And he brought him to a tailor in his father's city.

And he washed himself with the water, and his face was changed. And he went to that tailor; and that tailor was in his father's employment. And he hired himself as a prentice to the tailor for a twelvemonth, just to watch the baby in another room. The tailor had twelve prentices. And the tailor did not recognise him, nor his brothers.

The eldest brother proposed to the youngest sister, whom the seer had saved from the dragon. And she said, 'No, I have sworn not to marry until my own one comes.' The middle son also proposed; she said, 'I will not, until my own one comes.'

So the eldest son married the eldest girl; the middle son married the middle girl; and they called the tailor to make them wedding garments, and gave him cloth.

And the emperor's son said, 'Give it me to make.'

'No, I won't, you wouldn't fit him properly.'

'Give it me. I'll pay the damage if I don't sew it right.'

The tailor gave it him, and he rubbed the ring. Out came a little lord, and said, 'What do you want, master?'

'Take this cloth, and go to my eldest brother, and take his measure, so that it mayn't be too wide, or too narrow, but just an exact fit. And sew it so that the thread mayn't show.'

And he sewed it so that one couldn't tell where the seam came. And in the morning he brought them to the tailor.

'Carry them to them.'

And when they saw them, they asked the tailor, 'Who made these clothes? For you never made so well before.'

'I've a new prentice made them.'

'Since the youngest would not have us, we'll give her to him, that he may work for us.'

They went and got married. After the wedding they called the prentice, called too the maiden, and bade her go to him.

She said, 'I will not,' for she did not know him.

The emperor's eldest son caught hold of her to thrash her.

She said, 'Go to him I will not.'

'You've got to.'

'Though you cut my throat, I won't.'

Said the youngest son, 'I'll tell you what, Prince, let me go with her into a side-room and talk with her.'

He took her aside, and washed himself with the other water, and his face became as it was. She knew him.

'Come, now I'll have you.'

He washed himself again with the first water, and his face was changed once more, and he went back to the emperor. And he asked her, 'Will you have him?'

'I will.'

'The wedding is to be in twelve days.'

And they called the old tailor, and commanded him, 'In twelve days' time be ready for the wedding.' And they departed home.

Six days are gone, and he takes no manner of trouble, but goes meanly as ever. Now ten are gone, and only two remain. The tailor called the bridegroom. 'And what shall we do, for there's nothing ready for the wedding?'

'Ah! don't fret, and fear not: God will provide.'

Now but one day remained; and he, the bridegroom, went forth, and rubbed the ring. And out came a little lord and asked him, 'What do you want, master?'

'In a day's time make me a three-story palace, and let it turn with the sun on a screw, and let the roof be of glass, and let there be water and fish there; the fish swimming and sporting in the roof, so that the lords may look at the roof, and marvel what magnificence is this. And let there he victuals and golden dishes and silver spoons, and one cup being drained and one cup filled.'

That day it was ready.

'And let me have a carriage and six horses, and a hundred soldiers for outriders, and two hundred on either side.'

On the morrow he started for the wedding, he from one place, and she from another; and they went to the church and were married, and came home. His brothers came and his father, and a heap of lords. And they drink and eat, and all kept looking at the roof.

When they had eaten and drunk, he asked the lords, What they would do to him who seeks to slay his brother?'

His brothers heard. 'Such a one merits death.'

Then he washed himself with the other water, and his face became as it was. Thus his brothers knew him. And he said, 'Good day to you, brothers. You fancied I had perished. You have pronounced your own doom. Come out with me, and toss your swords up in the air. If you acted fairly by me, it will fall before you, but if unfairly, it will fall on your head.'

The three of them tossed up their swords, and that of the youngest fell before him, but theirs both fell on their head, and they died.

The Prince, his comrade and Natasa the Fair

No. 24.--The Prince, his Comrade, and Nastasa the Fair

There was an emperor with an only son; and he put him to school, to learn to read. And he said to his father, 'Father, find me a comrade, for I'm tired of going to school.' The emperor summoned his servants, and sent them out into the world to find a boy, and gave them a carriageful of ducats, and described what he was to be like, and how old. So they traversed all the world, and found a boy, and gave a carriageful of ducats for him, and brought him to the emperor. The emperor clothed him, and put him to the school; and he was the better scholar of the two.

There was an empress, the lovely Nastasa. A virgin she, who commanded her army. And she had a horse, which twelve men led forth from the stable; and she had a sword, which twelve more men hung on its peg. And princes came to seek her, and she said, 'He who shall mount my horse, him will I marry, and he who shall brandish my sword.' And when they led forth the steed, and the suitors beheld it, they feared, and departed home.

The emperor's son said, 'Father, I will go to Nastasa the Fair, to woo her'; and he said, 'Come with me, brother.' Their father gave them two horses, and gave them plenty of ducats; and they set out to Nastasa the Fair. And night came upon them, and they rested and made a fire.

And the emperor's son said, 'If I had Nastasa the Fair here, I would stretch myself by her side; and if her horse were here, what a rattling I'd give him; and if her sword were here, I would brandish it.'

And his brother said, 'All the same, you've got to feed swine.'

And in the morning they journey till night, and at night they rested again. Again he said, 'If I had Nastasa the Fair here, I would stretch myself by her side; and if her horse were here, I would rattle him; and if her sword were here, I would brandish it.'

'Brother, you've got to feed swine.'

He cut off his head with his sword, and went onward. And two Huculs came, and put his head on again, and sprinkled the water of life. And he arose, and mounted his horse, and gave each of the Huculs a handful of ducats. And he went after his brother, and caught him up on the road. And they journeyed till night, and he said to his brother, Brother, if you will hearken to me, it will go well with you.'

'I will, brother.' He came to Nastasa the Fair.

What have you come for?'

'We have come to demand your hand.'

And she said, 'Good, but will you mount my steed?'

'I will.'

She cried to her servants, 'Bring forth the steed.'

Twelve men brought him forth; the comrade mounted him. The horse flew up aloft with him, to cast him down. And he took his club, and kept knocking him over the head.

The horse said, 'Don't kill me.'

'Let yourself gently down with me, and fall beneath me, and I will take you by the tail and drag you along the ground, that she may see how I treat you.'

He cried aloud, 'What a poor, wretched horse you have given me. Bring the sword, that I brandish it.'

Twelve men brought the sword; he brandished it, and flung it to the Ninth Region. There was Paul the Wild; he was nailed to the roof by the palms of his hands. And thither he flung the sword; it cut off his hands, and he fled away.

They summoned the prince to table to eat, and set him at table, and twelve servants ate with him. They kept squeezing him, and he said, 'I'll step outside into the fresh air.' He went out, and said to his brother, 'Come, do you sit here, for I'm off.'

So he sat there in their midst, and they kept squeezing him. And he took his club, and began to lay about with it.

And he said, 'This is your way of showing one honour.' They fled and departed.

At nightfall now it grew dark, and Nastasa the Fair called the prince to her. He went to her. She set her foot on him, and picked him up, and he was like to die.

And he said, 'Let me go into the fresh air.'

She said, 'Go.'

He went out, and said to his brother, 'Stay you here, for I'm off.'

And he went and lay down beside her. She set her foot on him. He took his club and thrashed her with it, so that he left in her only the strength of a mere woman.

He went out, went to his brother. 'Well, brother, now you can go, and don't be frightened; but, when you come to her, give her a slap.'

He went to her, gave her a slap, and slept beside her. In the morning they went out for a walk, and she said to him, 'My lord, what a thrashing you gave me! yet when you came back you kissed me.'

And he said to her, 'I didn't kiss you, I gave you a slap.'

'Who then was it thrashed me?'

'My brother.'

She said not a word.

The brother slept by himself in another room. And she took the sword and cut off his feet. He made himself a winged cart; it ran a mile when he gave it a shove. And he found Paul the Wild, and said, 'Where are you going to, brother?'

'I am going into the world to get my living, for I have no hands.'

'Ha! let's become Brothers of the Cross, and do you yoke yourself to the cart, and draw it gently, for you have feet.'

They went a-begging, and went into the woods and found a house, and took up their abode in it. And they went into a city and begged. A girl came to give him an alms; and he caught her, and threw her into the cart, and fled with her into the forest, there where their house was. And they swore they would not commit sin with her. The devil came, and lay with her. And they heard, and arose in the morning.

And Dorohýj Kúpec asked, 'You swore. Why then did you go in to her and commit sin?'

'It wasn't me, brother, for I too heard, and I thought it was you.'

'He'll come this night, and do you take me in the stumps of your hands, and fling me on to them; I'll seize him, whoever he is.'

At night he came to her, and lay with her. They heard, and Paul took him and flung him on to them. He seized the devil, and they lit the candle, and began to beat him. And he prayed them not to, 'for I will restore you your feet, and likewise him his hands.' In the morning they bound him by the neck, and led him to a spring.

'Put your feet in the spring.'

He put his feet in the spring, and his feet became as they were before. And Paul put his hands in, and his hands were likewise restored. And Dorohýj Kúpec put some of the water of life in one pail, and some of the water of death in another. And he came back to their house; and they made a fire, put a fagot of wood on the fire, and burnt the devil, and flung his ashes to the wind. And Dorohýj Kúpec said, 'Now, brother, do you take that girl to yourself, and live with her, for I will go to my brother.'

He set out, and went to his brother, and found his brother by the roadside feeding swine.

'Well, do you mind my telling you, brother, you'd come to feed swine? Do you put on my clothes, and give me yours, for I'll turn swineherd, and do you stay behind.'

He took and drove the swine home, and she cried, 'Why have you driven the swine home so soon?'

The swine went into the sty, and one wouldn't go; and he took a cudgel and beat it so that it died. And when Nastasa the Fair saw that, she fled into the palace, for this is Dorohýj Kúpec.'

He followed her into the palace, and said to her, 'Good day to you, sister-in-law.'

'Thanks,' said she.

He caught her by the hand and dragged her out, and cut her all in pieces, and made three heaps of them; and two heaps he gave to the dogs, and they devoured them. And the rest of her he gathered into a single heap, and made a woman, and sprinkled her with the water of death, and she joined together; and sprinkled her with the water of life, and she arose.

'Take her, brother; now you may live with her, for now she has no great strength. I will go home,' said Dorohýj Kúpec.

And home he went.

The hen that laid diamonds

No. 25.--The Hen that laid Diamonds

There was a poor man, and he had three sons. And the youngest found six kreutzers, and said, 'Take, father, these six kreutzers, and go into the town and buy something.' And the old man went into the town and bought a hen, and brought it home; and the hen laid a diamond egg. And he put it in the window, and it shone like a candle. And in the morning the old man arose and said, 'Wife, I will go into the town with this egg.' And he went into the town, and went to a merchant. 'Buy this egg.'

'What do you want for it?'

'Give me a hundred florins.'

He gave him a hundred florins. The old man went home and bought himself food, and put the boys to school. And the hen laid another egg, and he' brought it again to that merchant, and he gave him a hundred more florins. He went home. Again the hen laid an egg; he brought it again to that merchant. And on the egg there was written: 'Whoso eats the hen's head shall be emperor; and whoso eats the heart, every night he shall find a thousand gold pieces under his head; and whoso eats the claws shall become a seer.'

The merchant came to that village and hired the old man: 'What shall I give you to convey my merchandise?'

'Give me a hundred florins.'

And he hired the man with the hen for half a year. The merchant came to the man's wife and said, 'Your man is dead, and my money is gone with him, but I'm willing to wed you: I'm rich.'

'Wedded let us be.'

'Good, we will, and kill me the hen for the wedding-feast. We shall do without fiddlers.'

And they hired a cook. 'Have the hen ready against our return from church.'

The boys came home from school. 'Give us something to eat.'

'I've nothing to give you, for he told me not to give any of the hen.'

And the boys begged her, 'Do let us have a bit too, for it was we looked after the hen; do let us have a bit too, if it's ever so little.'

She gave the eldest the head, and the middle one the heart, and to the youngest she gave the claws. And they went off to school.

And they came from the wedding, and sat down to table; and he said to the cook, 'Give us to eat.'

And she served up the hen to them. And he asked for the head and the heart, and he asked for the claws. There were none!

And he asked the cook, 'Where is the head?'

She said, 'The boys ate it.'

And he, that merchant, said, 'I don't want any of this hen. Give me the head and the heart and the claws; I will eat only them.'

The cook said, 'The boys ate them.'

And he said, 'Wife, make them bitter coffee to make them vomit.'

And they came home from school, and the youngest boy said, 'Don't drink this coffee, it will kill you.'

They went home, and their mother gave them the coffee; and they poured it on the ground and went back to school.

The merchant came and asked, 'Were they sick?'

She answered, 'No.'

'I will go to the town and buy apples; and do you entice them into the cellar, and I will cut their throats, and take out head, heart, and claws, and eat them.'

The youngest brother said, 'Let us go out into the world.'

'Go! what for?'

'Our father is meaning to kill us.'

They departed, and went into another kingdom. The emperor there was dead; and they took his crown and put it in the church; whosever head the crown falls on he shall be emperor. And men of all ranks came into the church; and the three boys came. And the eldest went before, and slipped into the church; and the crown floated on to his head.

'We have a new emperor.'

They raised him shoulder-high, and clad him in royal robes. A mandate is issued: There is a new emperor. The army came and bowed before the new emperor.

And the middle brother said, 'I'm off. I shan't stay here. I want to be emperor too.'

And the youngest said, 'I shall stay.'

So the middle one departed, and went to another emperor; that emperor had a daughter. And thus said the emperor, 'Whoever surpasses her in money, he shall marry her.'

He went to her. 'Come, let us play for money.'

They started playing; he beat her. One day they played, and two not. And he surpassed her in money, and wedded her. And the emperor joined them in marriage, and made him king.

And she had a lover. And that lover sent her a letter: 'Ask him where he gets all his money from.'

And she asked him: 'My lord, where do you get all your money from, that you managed to beat me?'

'Every night I find a thousand gold pieces under my head.'

'How so?'

'I ate a hen's heart.'

She wrote a letter and sent it to her lover: 'He ate a hen's heart, and every night he finds a thousand gold pieces under his head.'

And he sent her another letter: 'Make him coffee, that he vomit--vomit that heart up. And do you take it and eat it; then I'll marry you.'

She made him coffee, and he drank it, and vomited up the heart; and she took it and ate it. And she went to her father. 'Come, father, see how he vomits. He's not the man for me.'

The emperor saw how he vomited. 'Here, off you go. I don't want your sort.' And he took all his clothes off him, and gave him common clothes. And he departed.

He went into the forest, and he hungered, and he came to an apple-tree. He took an apple and ate it, and became an ass. He goes weeping, goes onward, and found a crab-apple, and ate one of its apples, and became a man again.

He turned back and took two apples, and took two also of the crab-apples, and went to the city where his wife was. And he stood by the roadside, and his wife went out to walk.

'Are your apples for sale, my man?'

'They are.'

He sold her an apple. She took a bite of it, and became a she-ass. He took her by the mane, and put a bridle on her head, and got on her, and galloped with her into the town, and went with her to an inn, and ordered bitter coffee, and poured it into her mouth; and she vomited, and vomited, and vomited up the heart. And he took it and ate it, and said, 'Now, I'm master.' And he went to his father-in-law: 'I demand justice; this is your daughter.'

The emperor summoned his ministers, but he said, 'I don't want *you* to pass judgment; come with me to the new emperor.'

So they went to the new emperor. And the emperor drives in his carriage, and he goes riding on his wife.

And the youngest brother said, 'My brother will appeal to you for judgment; deliver a good one.'

The emperors met, and bowed themselves; and the father-in-law said, 'Deliver judgment for this man.'

'I will. You have made her a she-ass; make her a woman again.'

'But she'll have to behave herself in the future.'

'She shall,' said her father, 'only do restore her.'

He gave her a crab-apple, and she ate it, and became a woman again. The emperor took off his crown and set it on his head. 'Do you take my crown, do you be emperor.'

No. 26.--The Winged Hero

There was a certain great craftsman, and he was rich. He took to drinking and gambling, and drank away all his wealth, and grew poor, so that he had nothing to eat. He saw a dream, that he should make himself wings; and he made himself wings, and screwed them on, and flew to the Ninth Region, to the emperor's castle, and lighted down And the emperor's son went forth to meet him, and asked him, 'Where do you come from, my man?'

'I come from afar.'

'Sell me your wings.'

'I will.'

'What do you want for them?'

'A thousand gold pieces.'

And he gave him them, and said to him, 'Go home with the wings, and come back in a month's time.'

He flew home, and came back in a month; and the prince said to him, 'Screw the wings on to me.'

And he screwed them on, and wrote down for the prince which peg he was to turn to fly, and which peg he was to turn to alight. The prince flew a little, and let himself

She was lying lifeless on the bed

down on the ground, and gave him another thousand florins more, and gave him also a horse, that he might ride home. The prince screwed on the wings, and flew to the south. A wind arose from the south, and tossed the trees, and drove him to the north. In the north dwelt the wind, drove him to the Ninth Region. And a fire was shining in the city. And he lighted down on the earth, and unscrewed his wings, and folded them by his side, and came into the house. There was an old woman, and he asked for food. She gave him a dry crust, and he ate it not. He lay down and slept. And in the morning he wrote a letter for her, and gave her money, and sent her to a cookshop with a letter to the cookshop to give him good food. And the old woman came home, and gave him to eat, and he also gave to the old woman. He went outside, and saw the emperor's palace with three stories of stone and the fourth of glass. And he asked the old woman, 'Who lives in the palace? and who lives in the fourth story?'

'The emperor's daughter lives there. He won't let her go out. He gives her her food there by a rope.'

And the maid-servant lowered the rope, and they fastened the victuals to it, and she drew them up by the rope. And the maid-servant had a bedchamber apart, where she slept only of a night, and the day she passed with the princess.

And that emperor's son screwed on his wings and flew up, flew to the glass house, and he looked to see how the bars opened, and opened them, and let himself in. And she was lying lifeless on the bed. And he shakes her, and she never speaks. And he took the candle from her head; and she arose, and embraced him, and said to him, 'Since you are come to me, you are mine, and I am yours.' They loved one another till daybreak; then he went out, placed the candle at her head, and she was dead. And he closed the bars again, and flew back to the old woman.

Half a year he visited the princess. She fell with child. The maid-servant noticed that she was growing big, and her clothes did not fit her. She wrote a letter to the emperor: 'What will this be, that your daughter is big?' The emperor wrote back a letter to her: 'Smear the floor at night with dough, and whoever comes will leave his mark on the floor.' She placed the candle at her head, and the girl lay dead. And she smeared the floor with dough, and went to her chamber. The emperor's son came again to her, and let himself in to her, and never noticed they had smeared the floor, and made footprints with his shoes, and the dough stuck to his shoes, but he never noticed it, and went home to the old woman, and lay down and slept. The servant-maid went to the emperor's daughter, and saw the footprints, and wrote a letter to the emperor, and took the measure of the footprints, and sent it to the emperor. The emperor summoned two servants, and gave them a letter, and gave them the measure of the footprints. 'Whose shoes the measure shall fit, bring him to me.' They traversed the whole city, and found nothing.

And one said, 'Let's try the old woman's.'

And another said, 'No, there's nobody there.'

'Stay here. I'll go.'

And he saw him sleeping, and applied the measure to his shoes. They summoned him. 'Come to the emperor.'

'All right.'

He bought himself a great cloak, and put it on, so that his wings might not be noticed, and went to the emperor. The emperor asked him, 'Have you been going to my daughter?'

'I have.'

'With what purpose have you done so?'

'I want to marry her.'

The emperor said, 'Bah! you'll not marry her, for I'll burn you both with thorns.'

The emperor commanded his servants, and they gathered three loads of thorns, and set them on fire, and lowered her down, to put them both on the fire. The emperor's son asked, 'Allow us to say a *pater noster*.' He said to the girl, 'When I fall on my knees, do you creep under the cloak and clasp me round the neck, for I'll fly upwards with you.'

She clasped him round the neck, and quickly he screwed the wings, and flew upwards. The cloak flew off, the soldiers fired their guns at it; on he flew. She cried, 'Let yourself down, for I shall bear a child.'

He said, 'Hold out.'

He flew further, and alighted on a rock on a mountain, and she brought forth a child there. She said, 'Make a fire.' He saw a fire in a field afar off. He screwed his wings, and flew to the fire, and took a brand of it, and returned. And a spark fell on one wing, and the wing caught fire. Just as he was under the mountain the wing fell off, and he flung away the other one as well. And he walked round the mountain, and could not ascend it.

And God came to him and said, 'Why weepest thou?' Ah! how should I not weep? for I cannot ascend the mountain, and my wife has brought forth a child.'

'What will you give me if I carry you up to the top?'

'I will give you whatever you want.'

'Will you give me what is dearest to you?'

'I will.'

'Let us make an agreement.'

They made one. God cast him into a deep sleep, and her as well, and God bore them home to his father's, to his own bed, and left them there, and departed. And the child cried. The warders heard a child crying in the bedchamber. They went and opened the door, and recognised him, the emperor's son. And they went to the emperor and told him, Your son has come, O emperor.'

'Call him to me.'

They came to the emperor; they bowed themselves before him; they tarried there a year. The boy grew big, and was playing one day. The emperor and the empress went to church, and his nurse too went to the church. God came, disguised like a beggar. The emperor's son said to the little lad, 'Take a handful of money, and give it to the beggar.'

The beggar said, 'I don't want this money; it's bad. Tell your father to give me what he vowed he would.'

The emperor's son was angry, and he took his sword in his hand, and went to the old man to kill him. The old man took the sword into his own hand and said, 'Give me what you swore to me--the child, you know--when you were weeping under the mountain.'

'I will give you money, I will not give you the child.'

God took the child by the head, and the father took him by the feet, and they tugged, and God cut the child in half.

'One half for you, and one half for me.'

'Now you've killed him, I don't want him. Take him and be hanged to you.'

God took him, and went outside, and put him together; and he was healed, and lived again.

'Do you take him now.'

For God cut off his sins.

NO. 27.--TROPSYN

There was a poor man, and he had four sons. And they went out to service, and went to a gentleman to thrash wheat. And they received so much wheat for a wage, and brought it to their father. 'Here, father, eat; we will go out to service again.' And they went again to a gentleman, who was to. give them each a horse at the year's end. And the youngest was called Tropsyn; and the gentleman made him his groom. And a mare brought forth a colt; and that colt said, 'Tropsyn, take me. The year is up now.'

The gentleman said, 'Choose your horses.'

So the three elder brothers chose good horses; but Tropsyn said, 'Give me this horse, master.'

'What will you do with it? it's so little.'

'So it may be.'

Tropsyn took it and departed; and the colt said, 'Let me go, Tropsyn, to my dam to suck.'

And he let it go, and it went to its dam, and came back a horse to terrify the world.

'Now mount me.'

In that meadow they saw the light of a fire

He mounted, and the horse flew. He caught up his brothers, and his brothers asked him, 'Where did you get that horse from?'

'I killed a gentleman, and took his horse.'

'Let's push on, and escape.'

Night fell upon them as they were passing a meadow, and in that meadow they saw the light of a fire. They made for the light. It was an old woman's, and she was a witch, and had four daughters. And they went there, and went into the house; and Tropsyn said, 'Good-night.'

'Thank you.'

'Can you give us a night's lodging?'

'I'm not sure; my mother is not at home. When she comes you had better ask her.'

The mother came home. 'What are you wanting, young fellows?'

'We've come to demand your daughters in marriage.'

'Good.'

She made them a bed on the ground with its head to the threshold, and her daughters' with its head to the wall. And the old woman sharpened her sword to cut off their heads. And Tropsyn took his brothers' caps, and put them on the girls' heads. And the old woman arose, and kept feeling the caps, and keeps cutting off the heads, and killed her daughters.

Tropsyn arose, and led his brothers outside. 'Come, be off.' And he arose, Tropsyn; and the old woman had a golden bird in a cage; and Tropsyn said to the horse, 'I will take a feather of the bird.'

And the horse said, 'Don't.'

'Bah! I will.' And he took a feather, and put it in his pocket.

And they mounted their horses and rode away, and went to a city. There was a great lord, a count; and he asked them, 'Where are you going?'

'We are going to service.'

'Take service with me, then.'

And that lord was still unmarried. And they went to him, and he gave them each a place. One he set over the horses, and one he set over the oxen, and one he set over the swine; and Tropsyn he made coachman. Of a night Tropsyn stuck the feather in the wall, and it shone like a candle. And his brothers were angry, and went to their master. 'Master, Tropsyn has a feather, such that one needs no candle--of gold.'

The master called: 'Tropsyn, come here, bring me the feather.'

Tropsyn brought it, and gave it to his master. The master liked him better than ever, and the brothers went to the master, and said to him, 'Master, Tropsyn has said that he'll bring the bird alive.'

The master called Tropsyn. 'Tropsyn, bring me the bird. If you don't, I shall cut off your head.'

He went to his horse. 'What am I to do, horse, for the master has told me to bring the bird?'

'Fear not, Tropsyn; jump on my back.'

So he mounted the horse, and rode to the old woman's. And the horse said to him, 'Turn a somersault, and you'll become a flea, and creep into her breast and bite her. And she'll fling off her smock, and do you go and take the bird.'

And he took the bird, and departed to his master; the master made him a lackey.

And there was in the Danube a lady, a virgin; and of a Sunday she would go out on the water in a boat. And his brothers came to their master and said, 'Master, Tropsyn boasts that he'll bring the lady from the bottom of the Danube.'

'Tropsyn, come here. What is this you've been boasting, that you'll bring me the lady?'

'I didn't.'

'You've got to, else I shall cut off your head.'

He went to his horse. 'What am I to do, horse, for how shall I bring her?'

And the horse said, 'Fear not, let him give you twelve hides and a jar of pitch, and put them on me, and let him make you a small ship, not big, and let him put various drinks in the ship. And do you hide yourself behind the door. And she will come, and drink brandy, and get drunk, and sleep. And do you seize her, and jump on my back with her, and I will run off home.'

The horse ran home to the master, and Tropsyn gave her to his master in the castle. The count shut the doors, and set a watch at the window to prevent her escape, for she was wild. The count wanted to marry her; she will not.

Let them bring my herd of horses, then I will marry you. He who brought me, let him bring also my horses.'

The count said, 'Tropsyn, bring the horses.'

Tropsyn went to his horse. 'What am I to do, horse? How shall I bring the horses from the Danube?'

'Come with me, fear not.'

When he came to the Danube, the horse leapt into the Danube, and caught the mother of the horses by the mane, and led her out. And Tropsyn caught her, and mounted her, and galloped off. And the whole herd came forth, and ran after their dam home to the count's palace. The lady cried ' Halt!' to the horses.

The count wants to marry her. She says, 'Let him milk my mares, and when you have bathed in their milk, then I will marry you.'

The count cried, 'Tropsyn, milk the mares.'

And Tropsyn went to his horse. 'What shall I do, horse? How shall I milk the mares?'

'Fear not, for I will catch her by the mane, and do you milk, and fear not.'

And he milked a whole caldron full.

And the lady said, 'Make a fire, and boil the milk.'

And they made a fire, and the milk boils.

'Now,' said the lady, 'let him who milked the mares bathe in the milk.'

And the count said, 'Tropsyn, go and bathe in the milk.'

He went to the horse. 'What shall I do, horse? for if I bathe, then I shall die.'

The horse said, 'Fear not, lead me to the caldron; I will snort through my nostrils, and breathe out frost.'

He led the horse; the horse snorted through his nostrils; then the milk became lukewarm. Then he leapt into the caldron, and fair as he was before, he came out fairer still. When he came out, the horse snorted through his nostrils, and breathed fire into the caldron, and the milk boiled again.

And the lady said to the count, 'Go thou too and bathe in the milk, then will I live with thee.'

The count went to the caldron and said, 'Tropsyn, bring me my horse.'

Tropsyn brought him his horse; the horse trembled from afar. The count leapt into the caldron; only bones were to be seen at the bottom of the caldron.

Then cried the lady, 'Come hither, Tropsyn; thou art my lord, and I am thy lady.'

No. 28.--The Beautiful Mountain

Somewhere far off were a quarryman and his wife. They had a son in their old age. They died. An old man comes to beg, and asks boy will he come with him to seek fortune. They go.

'Wish me into a horse.' Boy does so. 'Jump on my back.' He does so. They take the road. Horse warns boy to help anything in distress. Boy finds a little fish cast up by the tide, and puts it back in the water. Fish promises gratitude. They cross the Beautiful Mountain. Horse warns boy to touch nothing. A feather blows in his mouth. He spits it out again and again, but it returns. He looks at it, thinks it pretty, puts it in his pocket. They descend other side of the mountain. Boy hears noise of bellowing in a castle. Finds sick giant in bed, without servant-maid. Boy gets him food. Giant promises gratitude. Horse asks boy if he touched anything on mountain. 'Nothing but this feather.' 'That feather will bring you sorrow, but keep it now you have it.' They come to a castle. Boy asks for work. Master tests his hand-writing. Engages him. Wants him to sleep indoors; he prefers stable beside his old horse. They marvel at his penmanship, done with this feather. One day the master's man steals the pen by a ruse, and brings it to master: 'Master, the man that got the feather can get the bird.' Boy tells horse what they want him to do. Horse tells him to ask for three days' leave and three sacks of gold. Horse and boy go off. They go and get the bird, choosing the dirtiest and ugliest bird. The master's man says, 'Master, the bird is fair, but fairer still the lady' (that owned it). Boy told to fetch lady; he tells horse. Horse reminds him that he said the feather would bring him trouble. Three more days and three purses of gold. Horse says, 'Wish me into a boat on the sea.' The boat is full of the finest silk. They sail under the castle. Lure lady on board to see silk. She goes into cabin. Boy weighs anchor and off. Lady comes up, and drops her keys into sea. They return. Man says to master, 'Master, the man that got the lady can get the castle.' Boy tells horse. Horse reminds him of unlucky feather. Three more days and bags of gold. They go. Horse reminds boy of giant's promise. Giant puts chain round castle and drags it along. The castle is walled round and locked. Lady demands her keys. Boy and horse go off, call the little fish. He fails to find keys. Tries again and brings them up. Keys given to lady. Lady says, 'Which would you prefer, Jack, to have your head cut off or your master's head cut off?' Boy says, 'Cut off mine, not his.' Lady says, 'You have spoken well. Had you not spoken thus, your own head would have been cut off. Now the master's head will fall, not yours.' Boy and lady wed, and live in the castle still. 'Now you've got it.'

No. 29.--Pretty-face

There was a widow lady, and she had an only son. An he stuck his ring in the wall, and said, 'Mother, when blood flows from the ring, then I am dead.'

And he was called Peter Pretty-face.

He took the road, and the dragon with six heads came, and he drew his sword and killed him, and made three heaps of him, and planted a red flag, and went further. And a dragon with twelve heads came, and he drew his sword, and killed him also, and made twelve heaps, and planted a black flag, and went further. And there came one with twenty-four heads, and he killed him also, and made twenty-four heaps, and planted a white flag.

Behold! the dragons carried off an emperor's daughter--there were twelve dragons--and shut her up in their castle. And they went and fought from morning even till noon; he who shall prove himself strongest, he shall marry the maiden.

And his mother had said to him, 'If you will go, your death will not be by a hero, but your death will be by cripple.'

So he went to that castle, and saw the maiden at the window, and he asked her, 'What are you doing there?'

Peter Pretty Face attacked the dragons

'The dragons carried me off, and shut me up here.'

'And where are they gone to?'

'They are gone to fight for me.'

'And when will they come home?'

'They will come at noon to dine. And they will hurl their club, and it will strike the door, that I may have the food ready.'

He opened the door and went in to her. The dragon hurled the club, and struck the door; and he took the club and hurled it back, and killed them all.

'Now have no fear; they are dead.'

He married the emperor's daughter.

And the emperor heard that the dragons had carried off his daughter; and the emperor said, 'He who shall free her from the dragons, he shall marry her.' The emperor knew not that Peter Pretty-face had married her. He thought that the dragons had carried her off.

And there was one Chutilla the Handless, and he went to the emperor. 'I, O emperor, will rescue your daughter from the dragons.'

'Well, if you do, she shall be yours.'

So he, Chutilla, went to Peter Pretty-face. And night came upon him, and he had nowhere to sleep, and he crept into the hen-house. In the morning Peter Pretty-face arose, and washed his face, and looked out of the window, and Chutilla came forth from the hen-house.

And Peter Pretty-face saw him. ' By him is my death.' Chutilla came indoors and said, 'Good-morning, Peter Pretty-face.'

'Thanks, Chutilla.'

'Come, Peter Pretty-face, give me the emperor's daughter.'

He said, 'I will not.'

Chutilla caught him by the throat, and placed his head on the threshold. 'Give me, Peter Pretty-face, the maiden, else I will cut off your head.'

'Cut it off; I will not give her.'

Chutilla cut off his head, and took the girl and departed.

Blood began to flow from the ring. His mother saw it. 'Now my son is dead.' She went after him, to seek for him, and came to the red flag. His mother said, 'My son went this way.' She went further, and came to the black flag. 'My son went this way.' She went further, and came to the white flag. 'My son went this way.' She came to the castle, found her son dead; and two serpents were licking the blood. And she struck one serpent, and it died. And the other serpent brought a leaf in its mouth, and went to the first serpent, and it also arose. And the lady saw, and killed it also, and took the leaf, and placed her son's head again on the trunk, and touched it with the leaf, and he arose.

'Mother, I was sleeping soundly.'

'You would have slept for ever if I had not come.'

'Mother, I will go to my lady.'

'Go not, mother's darling.'

'Bah! I will go, mother.'

'If go you will, God aid you.'

He went, and went straight to Chutilla, and seized Chutilla, and cut him all in little pieces, till he had cut him up, and cast him to the dogs, and they devoured him. And he took the emperor's daughter, and went with her to the emperor.

And the maiden said, 'Father, this is he that saved me from the dragons.'

The emperor joined them in marriage, and made him king. And they live, perhaps they are living even now.

NO. 30.--THE RICH AND THE POOR BROTHER

There were two brothers, one poor and one rich. And the rich one said to him, 'Come with me, brother, to our father.' And the rich one took bread for himself, and the poor one had none.

And the rich one kept eating bread, and the poor one said, 'Give me, too, a bit of bread.'

'If you will give me an eye, I will give you a bit of bread.' 'I will give it you, brother.'

And he took out an eye, and gave him a bit of bread.

And he went further, and he hungered. 'Give me a bit more bread.'

'Give me one more eye.'

'I will give it you, brother.'

Behold, he was blind now, and his brother took him by the hand and led him under the gallows, and left him there; and his brother departed. At nightfall came the devils, and perched on the gallows.

And the biggest devil asked, 'What hast done in the world? where wert walking?'

'I did--I stopped the water.'

'And thou, what hast thou done?'

'The emperor's daughter neither dies nor lives; she is just in torment.'

'And thou, what hast thou done?'

'I did--that a brother dug out a brother's eyes.'

'If he knew, there's a brook here, and if he washed himself, he would see.'

'If the townsfolk knew to go to the mountain and remove the stone, the water would flow again.'

And the third said, 'But if the emperor's daughter knew, under her bed there is a toad, and if she takes it out, and gets ready a bath, and puts the toad in the bath, and if they wash her, she would grow strong.'

Then the cocks crowed, and the devils departed.

So the man dragged himself to the brook, and kept feeling with his hand till he found the water. And he washed his face, and his eyes were restored to him. And he went into the city where they had stopped the water. 'What will you give me if I release the water?'

'What you want, we will give you.'

'Well, come with me to the mountain, take to you iron crowbars.'

So they went to the mountain, and raised the stone; and the water flowed plentifully.

'Well, now, what do you want, man, for releasing the water?'

'Give me a carriage and two horses and a carriage full of money.'

They gave them to him. He went to the emperor's daughter. 'What will you give me if I make her strong?'

'What you want, I will give you.'

'Set water on the fire to boil.'

And he went and took out the toad, and threw it into the bath; and they washed the emperor's daughter, and she grew stronger and fairer than ever.

'What do you want for making her strong and fair?'

'Give me two horses and a carriage full of money, and give me a driver home.'

So he went home, and sent the servant to his brother, to borrow a bushel. And his brother asked, 'What to do with the bushel?'

They washed the Emperor's daughter

'To measure money with.'

His brother gave him the bushel; and went himself and asked his brother, 'Where did you get it, the money, from, and the horses?'

'From there where you left me.'

'Lead me, too, thither to that place. I am sorry, brother.'

'Don't be sorry; you've just got to go. Well, come, brother.'

So they both went to the place where he dug out his eyes.

'Give me, brother, a bit of bread.'

'Give me an eye.'

He gave him an eye, and he gave him a bit of bread.

And they went further. 'Give me, brother, a bit more bread.'

'Give me one more eye.'

'I will, brother.'

So he gave him a bit more bread, and took him by the hand, and led him under the gallows, and left him there, and departed. At nightfall came the devils, and perched on the gallows. And the biggest devil asked, 'What have you done? where have you been to in the world?'

One said, 'Don't tell, for there was lately a blind man under the gallows, and he heard what we said. And he made himself eyes, and made the water run, and raised up the emperor's daughter. Stay, while I look under the gallows.'

And they found the blind man. 'There's a blind man here.' And they rent him all in pieces. Then the devils departed; the man was dead.

No. 31--The Three Brothers

There was, there was not, a lord; and he had three sons. And one was the eldest son, and he said to his father, 'We will go somewhere to seek a livelihood.'

'Well, go, my sons,' said their father.

When they went, he baked loaves for each one to put in his wallet. Then they went a long way, and the youngest had most bread. And that youngest brother said, 'Brothers mine, I cannot carry this wallet, so first we will eat from my wallet, brothers mine.'

When they had eaten, they then went a long way further, and then those two brothers ate, and gave not to the third. He now had nothing, and says, 'Brothers mine, why don't you give me to eat? You ate up mine, and now you don't give me to eat.'

'If you'll let one of your eyes be taken out, then we will give you to eat,' said the two elder brothers. And then they took out his eye, and then gave him to eat. When they had eaten, they went a long way further. And there again those two brothers eat, and the third one says, 'Why don't you give me to eat? Now you've taken my eye out, and yet give me nothing to eat.'

'If you'll let your other eye be taken out, then we will give you to eat.'

And he, the youngest, says, 'Just do with me what you will.'

Then they took out his eye; then they gave him to eat; then that eyeless one said, 'Lead me under the cross; maybe some one will give me something.'

They led him not under the cross, but under a gallows, and there hung a dead man. And then thither came three crows, and thus talked one with another:

And thither came three crows.....

'What's the news in your country?' thus they asked one of them. 'What's the news?'

'In my country there is no water.'

'And in your country what's the news?'

'There's a dew there, if a blind man rubs his eyes with it, he forthwith sees.'

'And in your third country what's the news?'

'In my country there is a princess sick.'

And then those three crows went to the lad, and then they asked him what he was doing under the gallows. And he said, 'My brothers brought me here.'

And then those three crows flew away. And that lad feels in the grass with his hands, then he put it on his eyes, then he moistened his eyes; forthwith he saw. And then that lad departed to the king. That lad was then the king's servant, and went then to a city, and went up above the city, and saw there such a great rock, and struck that rock as with a rod; forthwith the water came from the rock. And then that water flowed into the city, where there was no water, there flowed that water, and the people were greatly rejoiced. And then he, that lad, cried that the water will always flow; then were the people greatly rejoiced that that water was flowing.

And then that boy went to another city, and there was a sick princess. He went to that king, and asked him, 'What's this princess got?'

'What's she got! she's sick.'

'If you will give me her to wife, then I will help her,' said that lad to the king.

'Do but help her, then we will give you her to wife.'

When he had healed her, then he took her to wife; and then they held the bridal seven whole years. And then he became young king.

That young king said to his soldiers, 'Hark ye, soldiers, go after my two brothers.'

Then those soldiers went after those two brothers, and then they brought the brothers. Then that young king asks them, 'How many brothers had you?'

And they said, 'We are only two.'

The king says, 'Hah! were there ever more of you?'

Then those two brothers say, 'We were three.'

Then, 'What have you done with the third one?'

'Done with him! He demanded of us to eat, then we took out his eyes.'

Then, 'I am he,' thus did that young king say. 'Now, what am I to do with you?'

Those two brothers say, 'Lead us under that cross.'

He led them under that very cross. When he had led them, there came again those same three crows. When they had come, again they asked one another, 'What is the news in your country?'

'In my country now is the princess well.'

'And in your second country what is the news?'

'In my country now is much water.'

'And in your third country what is the news?'

'There now is no such dew as they rubbed the eyes with.'

Then those three crows came to those two lads, and then there those crows say, 'We will tear these two lads.' And they tore and devoured them. And then those three crows flew away, and flew into the sky.

NO. 32.--THE ENCHANTED CITY

There was a poor lad, and he served seven years, and could not earn anything. And he went into the world, and went into a city, and spent the night there, and lay down under a wall, and slept. In that wall there was a hole, and he awoke, and looked through the hole, and saw a candle. And he crept through the hole, and went into a palace. There was a great city, and there was an emperor in the city; and the emperor was dead, and also the empress was dead. And the emperor had a daughter, and she commanded the army. And that city was excommunicated, and the people were turned into stone. So the lad went into the palace of the emperor, and there in the palace all were turned into stone. And he marvelled what this might be, that the men were like men, but yet were all turned into stone.

A cat came, and set food on the table. He sat down to table, and ate. At night came the cat, and brought him food, and brought. him cards, and said to him, 'There will come a lord, and will say, "Play at cards," and do you play; and he will spit on you, and do you bear it, but look at the clock. When it strikes ten, then give him a slap.'

Then there came devils as many as the blades of grass; and they beat him and tormented him till twelve o'clock; and the cocks crowed, and they fled. He lay down in the bed and slept. In the morning the cat brought him food, and he ate. At nightfall she again brought him food, said to him, 'He will come again for you to play with him, and do you play till ten o'clock, and give him a slap; and they will come to you as many as all the blades of grass, and will beat you and torment you, and do you bear it till twelve o'clock.'

The lord came to him. 'Hah! let us play cards.'

And they played till ten o'clock. He gave him, the devil, a slap. They came as many as all the blades of grass, and they beat him and tormented him till twelve o'clock, and they fled. He lay down in the bed and slept. In the morning he heard the folks talking in the city. In the morning the cat brought him food, and brought him royal clothes. He ate, and put on the clothes, and went into twelve chambers. There was the emperor's daughter in her bed. One half was alive, and she said, 'You are my emperor, and I am your empress, but come no more to me.'

Again at night the cat brought him food, and said to him, He will come again to-night to play cards till ten o'clock. At ten o'clock give him a slap again, and they will come to you as many as all the blades of grass, and they will beat you and torment you, but bear it.'

That lord came to him. 'Hah! let us play cards.'

And they played till ten o'clock. He gave him a slap, and they came as many as all the blades of grass, and they beat him and tormented him, and he bore it till twelve o'clock. At twelve o'clock they fled. He lay down on the bed and slept. In the morning the band began to play, they held a review. 'For we have a new emperor.' The ministers came to him, and raised him shoulder-high. 'We have a new emperor.'

And he is in a hurry to go to his empress, and said, 'Stay here, I will be back immediately.'

And he went to her. There she stood with her head to the roof, and a vapour went forth from her mouth; and he opened the door, and she just made a sign to him with her hand, and fell back on the bed, and became stone up to the waist. And she called him to her. 'Leave me; I want you not. Why did you not wait to come to me, till I should obtain remission of my sins? Take you my father's horse and his sword, and take a purse; as much money as you want, it shall not fail.'

He set out, and journeyed, and departed into another kingdom. There two emperors were fighting, because one would not give his daughter to the other's son. 'Set yourself to battle with me, since you refuse your daughter.' They fought seven years. So he came into that city, and came to an inn, to a certain Armenian. And there was a great famine; the soldiers were dying of hunger. So he asked the Armenian, 'What's the news here?'

'No good. They have been waging a great war seven years here for a girl, and the soldiers are dying of hunger.' And he said, 'Go and call them to me.'

The soldiers came, and he bought bread and brandy, and they drank and ate; and he said to the Armenian, 'I, if I choose, I will cut that army to pieces.'

She laid him on the table and put him all together

The Armenian went to the emperor. 'Emperor, a king's son is come, and has boasted that he by himself will cut that army to pieces.'

'Call him to me.'

'What is this you've been boasting? will you cut that army to pieces?'

'I will.'

'If you do, I will give you my daughter, and give you one half of my kingdom.'

And he, when he went to battle, waved to the right hand, and slew one half of the army, and he waved to the left hand, and slew the other half. And he came home, and the emperor gave him his daughter, and made a marriage.

'Ask him what strength is his, that he slew so great an army.'

And he said, 'My sword slays.'

And she sent back a letter, 'The sword alone slays; send me another sword, and I will send this one to you.'

She sent him the sword, and he then said, 'Set yourself now to battle with me.'

And he went in hope. But the emperor slew him, and cut him all in pieces, and put him in the saddle-bags, and placed him on his horse, and said, 'Whence thou didst bear him living, bear him dead.'

The horse carried him home, thither to that lady who was of stone. She cried, 'Bring him to me.' She laid him on a table, and put him all together; and she sprinkled him with dead water, and he became whole; and she sprinkled him with living water, and he arose.

Go back; take you this purse, you have but to wish and you will find it full of money. And go to that Armenian, and give him whatever he wants, and tell him you will turn yourself into a horse. Take a hair from my tail, and bind it round you like a girdle, and fling a somersault.'

So he turned himself into a horse; and the Armenian took him, and led him into the city. The emperor bought him, and mounted him. He dashed him to the earth, and he died. The horse took the sword in his mouth, and went to the Armenian. The Armenian' loosened the hair, and he became a man again. He made the Armenian king; and he departed home to his mistress, the first one, and wedded her. And he became emperor.

No. 33.--The Jealous Husband

There was a merchant, great and wealthy, and he had a beautiful wife; he did not let her go out. And he went in a ship on the Danube after merchandise with another merchant. And they were coming home. They hauled their ships to the bank, and moored them to the bank, to pass the night. They fell into discourse. Said one, 'Has your wife got a lover at home?'

And he said, 'My wife has not got a lover.'

'Come, what will you give me if I become her lover?'

'If you do, I will give you my estate, and my merchandise too, ship and all.'

'How will you know that I am her lover?'

If you tell me her birth-mark, and if you take the gold ring from her finger. But my wife will be like to thrash you, if you but hint such a thing to her. I left a maid with her, to see that my wife does not go out of doors.'

'I shall succeed, though.'

'Go home and try; I'll bring your ship.'

Home he went. What will he do? for he cannot come near her. He found an old wife. 'Old wife, what am I to do to get the ring from the lady?'

'What will you give me if I contrive that you get it?'

'I will give you a hundred florins.'

'Get a big chest made, and a window in it, and get into it, and make a bolt inside, and I will carry you to her.'

She carried him in the chest under the wall of her house, and went to the lady. 'I beg you, lady, to take in my box of clothes, so that they may not be stolen.'

'Carry it into the hall.'

She called the maid, and the maid helped her to carry him into the hall.

'I beg you, lady, to let me take it right into your house. I will come in the morning to fetch it.'

'Well, put it in a corner.'

The old woman went off home. The lady at night took a bath, and laid the ring on the table, and washed herself. And through the little window he perceived a mole under her right breast. The lady slept all night in her bed, and forgot the ring on the table, and put out the candle. And he let himself out, took the ring off the table, and got back into the chest, shut himself in. The old woman came next morning at daybreak, and carried her chest outside. He opened it, and came out, and took the chest, and departed. He went to meet the husband, and found him on the way.

'Hast thou lain with my lady?'

I have.'

'What is her birth-mark?'

'She has a mole under her right breast. If you do not believe me, here is the ring as well.'

'It's all right; take the ship and everything in it, and come home, and I will give you also the estate.'

He went home, and said never a word to the lady; and he made a little boat, and put her in it, and let it go on the Danube. 'Since you have done this, away you go on the Danube.' He gave his whole estate, and became poor, and carried water for the Jews.

A whole year she floated on the Danube; the year went like a day. An old man caught her, and drew her to shore, and opened the boat, and took her out, and brought her to his house. She abode with him three years, and spun with her spindle, and made some money. And she bought herself splendid man's clothes, and dressed herself, and cut her hair short, and went back to her husband. She went and passed the night beneath a lime-tree, and slept under the lime-tree. In that city the emperor was blind. She saw a dream: in the lime-tree was a hole, and in the hole was water; and if the emperor will anoint himself with that water he will see. She arose in the morning, and

She saw her husband carrying water

searched around, and found the hole. And she had a little pail, and she drew water in the pail, and put it in her pocket, and went into that city to an inn, and drank three kreutzers' worth of brandy. And she asked the Jew, 'What's the news with you?'

'Our emperor is blind, and he will give his kingdom to him who shall make him see.'

'I will do so.'

The Jew went to the emperor, and the emperor said to him, 'Hah! go and bring him to me.'

They brought him to the emperor. 'Will you make me see? then I will give you my daughter.'

She took water, and anointed his eyes, and he saw. The emperor set his crown on her head. 'Do you be emperor. I want nothing but to stay beside you.' The emperor clad her royally, called his army, beat the drum. 'For there's a new emperor.'

And she saw her husband carrying water for the Jews. 'Come hither. Have you always been poor?'

'No, I once was not poor, I was rich. I had an estate, and I was a great merchant.'

'Then how did you lose your estate?'

'I lost it over a wager. My wife played the wanton with another, and I gave up the estate, and sent her adrift on the Danube.'

Straightway she sent for the other, and they brought him. 'How did you come by this man's estate?'

'Over a wager.'

'What was your wager?'

'That I would lie with her.'

'Then you did so?'

'I did.'

'And, pray, what were her birth-marks?'

'Under her right breast she had a mole.'

'Would you know that mole again?'

'I would.'

Then she drew out her breast. 'Did you lie with me?'

'I did not.'

'Then why those falsehoods? Here, take him, and cut him all to pieces.'

And she looked earnestly on her husband. 'You, why did you not ask me at the time?'

'I was a fool, and I was angry.'

Here, take him outside, and give him five-and-twenty, to teach him wisdom.'

She threw the robes off her, and put them on him. 'Do you be emperor, and I empress.'

Francis Hindes Groome

No. 34.--Made over to the Devil

There was a rich man, and he went into the forest, and fell into a bog with his carriage. And his wife brought forth a son, and he knew it not. And the Devil came forth, and said, 'What will you give me if I pull you out?'

I will give you what you want.'

'Give me what you have at home.'

'I have horses, oxen.'

'Give me that which you have not seen.'

'I will.'

'Make a covenant with me.'

He made a covenant with him, and the Devil pulled him out of the mud, and the man went home. By the time he got home he had forgotten the covenant.

The boy was twenty years old. 'Make me a cake, mother, for I'm off to the place my father pledged me to.' And he went far over the mountains, and came to the Devil's house. There was an old woman in the house, and a daughter of the Devil's, and she asked him, 'Whither art going, lad?'

'I have come to the lord here, to serve.'

And the girl saw him, and he pleased her. 'I may tell you that he is my father. My father will turn himself into a horse, and will tell you to mount him and traverse the world. And do you make yourself an iron club and an iron curry-comb, and hit him with the club, for he will not stoop, and get on his back, and as you go keep hitting him on the head.'

He traversed the world, and came home, put him in the stable, and went to the maiden.

'My father didn't fling you?'

'No, for I kept hitting him on the head.'

The Devil called him, and took a jar of poppy-seed, and poured it out on the grass, and told him to gather it all up, and fill the jar, for, 'If you don't, I will cut off your head.'

He went to the maiden, and wept.

'What are you weeping for?'

'Your father has told me to fill the jar with poppy-seed; and if I don't, he will cut off my head.'

She said, 'Fear not.' She went outside and gave a whistle, and the mice came as many as all the blades of grass and the leaves.

And they asked, 'What do you want, mistress?'

'Gather the poppy-seed and fill the jar.'

And the mice came and picked up the grains of poppy-seed one by one, and filled the jar.

The Devil saw it. 'You're a clever chap. Here is one more task for you: drain the marsh, and plough it, and sow it, and to-morrow bring me roasted maize. And if you do not, I shall cut your head off.'

He went to the maiden and wept. 'Your father has told me to drain the marsh, and give him roasted maize to-morrow.'

'Fear not.'

She went outside, and took the fiery whip. And she struck the marsh once, and it was dried up; a second time she struck, and it was ploughed; the third time she struck, it was sowed; the fourth time she struck, and the maize was roasted; and in the morning he gave him roasted maize.

She said to him, 'We are three maidens. He will make us all alike, will call you to guess which is the eldest, which is the middle one, and which the youngest; and you will not be able to guess, for we shall be all just alike. I shall be at the top, and notice my feet, for I shall keep tapping one foot on the other; the middle one will be in the middle, and the eldest fronting you, and so you will know.'

The Devil said to him, 'One more task I will give you. Fell the whole forest, and stack it by to-morrow.'

He went to the maiden, and the maiden asked him, 'Have you a father and mother?'

'I have.'

'Ah! let us fly, for my father will kill you. Take the whetstone, and take a comb; I have a towel.'

They set out and fled. The Devil arose, saw that the forest is not felled. ' Go and call him to me.'

Ho, ho! there is neither the lad nor the maiden.

'Hah! go after them.'

They went, and the two saw them coming after them. And she said to him, 'I will make myself a field of wheat, and do you make yourself to be looking at the wheat, and they will ask you, "Didn't a maiden and a lad pass by?" "Bah! they passed when I was sowing the wheat."'

'Go back, for we shall not catch them.'

They went back. 'We did not catch them.'

'On the road did not you find anything?'

'We found a field of wheat and a peasant.'

'Go back, for the field of wheat was she, and he was the peasant.'

They saw them again. She said to the lad, 'I will turn a somersault and make myself an old church, and do you turn a somersault and make yourself an old monk, and they will ask you, "Didn't a maiden and a lad pass by?" "They passed just as I began the church."'

'Ah! go back, for we shall never catch them. When he was beginning the church! It is old now.'

'Did you not find anything on the road?'

'We found a church and a monk.'

'The church was she, and he was the monk. I will go myself.'

They saw him. 'Now my father is coming; we shall not escape. Fling the comb.'

He flung the comb, and it became a forest from earth to sky. Whilst he was gnawing away the forest, they got a long way ahead. He was catching them up; she cried, Fling the whetstone.'

He flung the whetstone, and it became a rock of stone from earth even to heaven. Whilst he, the Devil, was making a hole in the rock, they got a long way ahead. Again he is catching them up. 'Father is catching us up.' She flung the towel, and it became a great water and a mill. They halted on the bank.

And he cried, 'Harlot, how did you cross the water?'

…whilst the Devil was making a hole in the rock…

'Fasten the millstone to your neck, and jump into the water.'

He fastened the millstone to his neck, and jumped into the water, and was choked.

She said, 'Fear not, for my father is choked.'

He went to his father with the maiden. His father rejoiced; but the maiden said to the lad, 'I will go to expiate my father's sins, for I choked him. I go for three years.'

She took her ring, and broke it in half, and gave one half to him. 'Keep that, and do not lose it.' She departed for three years.

He forgot her, and made preparations to marry. He was holding his wedding. She came, and he knew her not.

'Drink a glass of brandy.'

She drank out of his glass, and flung the half of the ring into the glass, and gave it to him. When he drank, he got it into his mouth, and he took it in his hand and looked at it, and he took his half and fitted the two together. 'Hah! this is my wife; this one saved me from death.'

And he quashed that marriage, and took his first wife and lived with her.

No. 35.--The Lying Story

Before I was born, my mother had a fancy for roast starlings. And there was no one to go, so I went alone to the. forest. And I found roast starlings in the hollow of a tree. I put in my hand, and could not draw it out. I took and got right in, and the hole closed up. I set out and went to my godfather to borrow the axe.

My godfather said, 'The servant with the axe is not at home, but,' said my godfather, 'I will give you the hatchet, and the hatchet is expecting little hatchets.'

'Never fear, godfather.'

And he gave me the hatchet, and I went and cut my way out of the tree, and I flung down the hatchet. Whilst it was falling a bird built its nest in the handle, and laid eggs, and hatched them, and brought forth young ones; and when the hatchet had fallen down, it gave birth to twelve little hatchets. And I put them in my wallet, and carried them to my godfather. My godfather rejoiced. He gave me one of the hatchets, and I stuck it in my belt at my back, and went home. I was thirsty and went to the well. The well was deep. I cut off my brainpan, and drank water out of it. I laid my brainpan by the well, and went home.

And I felt something biting me on the head; and when I put up my hand to my head there came forth worms. I returned to my brainpan, and a wild-duck had laid eggs in my brainpan, and hatched them, and brought forth ducklings. And I took the hatchet, and flung it, and killed the wild-duck, but the ducklings flew away. Behind the well was a fire, and the hatchet fell into the fire. I hunted for the hatchet, and found the handle, but the blade of the hatchet was burnt. And I took the handle, and stuck it in my belt at my back, and went home, and found our mare, and got up on her. And the handle cut the mare in half, and I went riding on two of her legs, and the two hind ones were eating grass. And I went back, and cut a willow withy, and trimmed it, and sewed the mare together. Out of her grew a willow-tree up to heaven. And I, remembered that God is owing me a treeful of eggs and a pailful of sour milk. And I climbed up the willow, and went to God, and went to God's thrashing-floor. There twelve men were thrashing oats.

'Where are you going to, man?'

'I am going to God.'

'Don't go; God isn't at home.'

And the smiths felled the willow, and I took an oat-straw and made a rope, and let myself down. And the rope was too short, and I kept cutting off above, and tying on below; then I jumped down, and came to the other world. I went home, and got a spade, and dug myself out [of the other, or nether world], and went home, and gave the starlings to my mother, and she ate, and was safely delivered of me, and I am living in the world.

No. 36.--Happy Boz'll

Wonst upon a time there was a Romano, and his name was Happy Boz'll, and he had a German-silver grinding-barrow, and he used to put his wife and his child on the top, and he used to go that quick along the road he 'd beat all the coaches. Then he thought this grinding-barrow was too heavy and clumsy to take about, and he cut it up and made tent-rods of it. And then his donkey got away, and he didn't know where it was gone to; and one day he was going by the tent, and he said to himself, 'Bless my soul, wherever's that donkey got to?' And there was a tree close by, and the donkey shouted out and said, 'I'm here, my Happy, getting you a bit o' stick to make a fire.' Well, the donkey come down with a lot of sticks, and he had been up the tree a week, getting firewood. Well then, Happy had a dog, and he went out one day, the dog one side the hedge, and him the other. And then he saw two hares. The dog ran after the two; and as he was going across the field, he cut himself right through with a scythe; and then one half ran after one hare, and the other after the other. Then the two halves of the dog catched the two hares; and then the dog smacked together again; and he said, 'Well, I've got 'em, my Happy'; and then the dog died. And Happy had a hole in the knee of his breeches, and he cut a piece of the dog's skin, after it was dead, and sewed it in the knee of his breeches. And that day twelve months his breeches-knee burst open, and barked at him. And so that's the end of Happy Boz'll.

Abela Publishing

Yesterday's Books

for

Today's Charities

www.AbelaPublishing.com

(Abela: Zulu – to share or distribute)

Lightning Source UK Ltd.
Milton Keynes UK
UKHW041808120219
337211UK00001B/11/P

9 781907 256073